The Museum of

Stories by
SYLVIA TOWNSEND WARNER

Critics appraising Sylvia Townsend Warner have compared her humor to Jane Austen's, her fantasy to David Garnett's, the polish of her prose with Elinor Wylie's in *The Venetian Glass Nephew.* The Sitwells, Katherine Mansfield, W. H. Davies, James Stephens, are other favorite comparisons. But in the end it is always acknowledged that she is in reality not "like" anyone else. The author of *Lolly Willowes* and *Mr. Fortune's Maggot* will always be herself.

Her acidly wise, sharply observing, cool and impeccable prose is for the connoisseur, although it is pleasant to note that her audience is far from small and united by a wish that she would write more frequently. *The Museum of Cheats,* the first collection of her stories in more than three years, is a fresh bouquet to gladden her readers. The long story which gives the book its title is an amazing tale of two and a half centuries in the life of an odd museum full of mermaids and relics and old tomes and an alchemical laboratory, subtly enmeshed in the history of the town and its people—many of them cheats. The other twenty-one stories evidence the variety of subject and the highly imaginative quality peculiar to Miss Warner. They range all the way from deceptively simple accounts of simple people to the slightly mad story of a schizophrenic primitive painter—from the gory to the gay.

Eleven of the twenty-two stories have appeared in *The New Yorker,* to whose distinguished pages the author has from time to time given additional luster.

The Museum of Cheats

Books by Sylvia Townsend Warner

NOVELS

After the Death of Don Juan

Summer Will Show

The True Heart

Mr. Fortune's Maggot

Lolly Willowes

SHORT STORIES

A Garland of Straw

The Cat's Cradle-Book

The Salutation

POEMS

Whether a Dove or Seagull (*With Valentine Ackland*)

Opus 7

Time Importuned

The Espalier

The Museum of Cheats

Stories by

SYLVIA TOWNSEND WARNER, 1893-

THE VIKING PRESS

New York · 1947

Published by The Viking Press in March 1947

Grateful acknowledgment is made to The New Yorker *in which the following stories originally appeared:* "*Poor Mary,*" "*The Cold,*" "*English Climate,*" "*Daphnis and Chloe,*" "*Bow to the Rising Sun,*" "*Story of a Patron,*" "*Sweethearts and Wives,*" "*The House with the Lilacs.*"

Printed in U. S. A.
by the Vail-Ballou Press, Inc., Binghamton, N. Y.

Contents

Contents

The Museum of Cheats

Poor Mary

AT THE last minute Nicholas remembered flowers. He went out and gathered some primroses from the hedgerow, hardening himself not to notice the snap of their stems. It was one of his fidgets to dislike picking flowers.

The lane sloped away downhill. Here and there the leafless hedge was tufted with white where the blackthorns had come into bloom. It was like a black wave breaking into lips of foam. Down in the valley a white plume of steam swelled up, its summit catching the pink light of sunset. It was still hanging there when he heard the train go on. And he knew that his wife, shouldering her pack, had handed in her pass and joined the nondescript civilian group waiting for the bus. The white plume thinned out, the train gathered speed, snorting on towards London. Mary had got out at East Wickering, junction for Stoat and Saint Brewers. *I want to spend this leave at home,* she had written, *unless you'd rather not. It's more than time I saw you in your hermit's cell.* If it had not been for the last sentence he would have supposed that she wanted to spend her leave with her family.

"Flowers for the spare room," he said to himself, setting down the spotted mug in the centre of the bureau. The bed, an old-fashioned double bed with brass end-rails and a white quilt, suddenly seemed a bed in which he had never slept. It looked like Wordsworth's bed. He must contrive that she saw the camp-bed first. For the last week he had spent his spare time preparing for her, scrubbing the floors, polishing the windows, putting away his clothes, his books, his papers, so that his dwelling might offer its most impersonal face to her inspection. Now that he had remembered flowers everything seemed ready. The food on the table was covered with a napkin to keep the flies off it, the kettle was in a state to boil when he wanted it to, the water cress was keeping cold in a damp cloth. He snuffed at his fingers' ends, and once more washed his hands very carefully. He had been cleaning out pigsties all the morning. Then he set off to meet his wife.

He had not seen her since 1941. A conscientious objector, he had applied for exemption from military service. The day after the tribunal had granted exemption provided that he worked on the land Mary had volunteered for the A.T.S. They had never agreed about war, so neither was surprised by the other.

"But as we are bound to argue," she had said, "and as people will only laugh at you if you have a military wife coming on visits, I shall not come. Unless you are ill, of course. Then I will apply for compassionate leave."

One of the things he had learned in his four years as

a farm labourer was an exact computation of time. So he met her where he had intended to meet her, fifty yards from where the bus had set her down at the foot of the lane. Though he knew she would be wearing uniform it was a surprise to see that part of the uniform was a skirt. He had been similarly astonished on their wedding day when apparently he had been assuming that she would walk up the aisle wearing white satin trousers. Seeing the skirt he also saw her legs below it and that they were fatter than they used to be.

"Hallo, Nicholas," she said.

"Hallo, Mary."

She smells of metal, he thought, as I smell of dung. We are subdued to what we work in. He had smelled her; he had seen her legs. He did not seem to have seen her face.

He took her pack and said: "Look! There's a hawk."

"I suppose they do a lot of harm to the crops," she replied.

"Wood-pigeons are worse," Nicholas said.

She set off, walking with quick resolute steps—marching, in fact. So why on earth should she know about hawks? The thought prompted an inquiry about the V-2, and they went up the lane talking of air raids and air-raid damage.

Just as there was a difference between their smells and in their gait, there was a difference in their manner of speech. Her voice had grown rather common and twanging, it sounded uncared for, and she jumped from one subject to another. She seemed to preface every remark with *Gosh!* and he to inaugurate every reply with *Um.* Listening to himself he thought: Do I sound more like the village schoolmaster or the village idiot?

A melancholy tenderness that was almost entirely the April dusk suffused him. Blackbirds shot across the lane from hedge to hedge, scolding at them. Beyond the hedges lambs bleated and rushed away at a ghostly gallop. He had been working since six in the morning, he was tired and craved for tea. Yet each time they paused for Mary to recover her breath he was glad to postpone the moment of reaching his house, and when the one chimney-pot reared into view above the hedge and beneath the evening star he said gloomily: "Here's where I live."

"It's nice. And all to yourself? Lucky bastard!"

"There are only two rooms," he said defensively. "The third one leaks."

"Is it old?"

"Run up after the last war by a chicken-farming ex-service man. When he was ruined the farmer bought it. As he bought it very cheap, naturally he doesn't trouble to keep it in repair. So I sit in the kitchen. But I've got a chemical closet."

It was strange to hear her feet on the floor of concrete slabs. Not strange to her, though, who had been living for four years in army constructions. The only strange thing to her would be to hear two pairs of feet instead of thirty. He moved the kettle forward on the range and lit the candles.

"Candles!" she said appreciatively.

"Because it's a party. Ordinarily I use an oil lamp." His voice was still heavy with gloom.

"What queer squat candlesticks! They're clay, aren't they? Did you make them?"

"No, I bought them at a sale. They're called corpse candlesticks. The idea is that you leave them by the body all night, you see, and the rats can't knock them over."

"I wonder you don't use them every night," she said. "Have you got any other cheerful curiosities?" She had taken off her cap and unbuttoned her tunic. The candle-light softened the contest between her natural high colour and the too tawny make-up she had applied to it.

Seeing that he was looking at her she said: "Isn't it calamitous how fat I've grown? It's that army food, incessant gorges of starch. Gosh! Those puddings! Enough to make any girl look like a prize ox."

"When I first came here I was covered with spots and boils," he said consolingly. "I thought I'd caught it from the pigs till I discovered it was my well. Now I boil it."

"I'd hate to have to do with pigs," she said.

"They're clean animals, really. It's just that they are overcrowded, and dirty feeders."

"Sounds like the A.T.S."

He cut more bread, reflecting that he would need to bake again on the morrow. Habit, of course, and mass feeding, and the goaded appetite of the disciplined, though that would not account for the scatteration of eggshell, the jam spooned on to a salted plate, the wide periphery of crumbs and cigarette ash. Nerves, he thought. Poor Mary's nerves are strained. His own strained nerves obliged him to sip his tea as though it were Napoleon brandy and frown at an iron mould on the cloth.

"Lovely bread, Nicholas."

"Soda bread. I bake it myself."

"You seem to have a lot of time. Don't you ever do any work?"

"Fifty-six hours a week. Sometimes overtime. Pigs on Sunday. But it fits in somehow, and I don't dislike it. And the alternative would be to have a woman in."

He had not meant the implication and she did not perceive it.

Staring round her as though in a foreign country she said: "And the polish on everything too! You're wasted, Nicholas. You ought to have been in the army."

"Yes, sergeant."

More concerned than he had been over his own maladroit remark, she flushed, and refused to eat anything more, like an abashed child.

"Walk round and see the rest of it. Here's your room."

"Pretty flowers."

Glaring at the bed he remarked: "I've got a bed in the third room."

"But that's the room that leaks. You said so."

She had turned around from the mirror, and it was as though the mirror had given back to her her former countenance, at once innocent and domineering, the face of the girl-child intent on the doll's tea-party.

"It doesn't leak in dry weather," he said. "I expect the cat's there now. She comes in and out by the window."

"Cat? Why, you used to hate cats. You said they tortured birds."

"So they do. So I do hate them. But I must needs find this one in a gin, and dress its paw, and the damned beast has adopted me. It's a female too."

"Life's harder in the country, I expect," she said.

It was for such slanting ironies that he had first loved her: for that, and for smelling of geraniums, and for the chivalrous, quarrelsome disposition which had kept her at his side before his exemption was assured, saying hopefully that he might need someone to scrap with the authorities.

But unseeing she went on to undo it by saying: "You know, a lot of people are awfully interested when I tell them that my husband is a C.O. You'd be surprised how many feel the same way. All these murder cases, you know. Everyone's dead against the death sentence."

"It doesn't surprise me very much," he said. "I was in the train the other day, I had to go to a dentist, and there was a bomber crew in the same carriage, and they were talking about a murder. They all agreed that it was wrong to take human life. I asked one of them why, and he said because you can't know what it is you're meddling with."

"Exactly! I've heard dozens say the same thing. I'm beginning to think so myself. I think they ought to abolish it. I expect they will after the war."

"They'll abolish war, my dear. Belligerents always abolish war after a war. It's harder to part with a death sentence. And impossible to give up hunting and shooting because hunting and shooting make us what we are. Have a cigarette?"

"I don't think you've grown any pleasanter," she said. "Is that an owl? Let's go back to the other room."

In the other room the clock was ticking, the kettle was boiling. Three hours earlier the bed had not seemed his own, now his kitchen was not his either, but some sort of institutional waiting-room where two people had made an inordinately messy meal. At last, irked beyond bearing, he rose and began to clear the table and then to wash up. The hot water in the bowl, the feeling of the crockery, dried and still warm as he stacked it on the dresser, the resumption of his ordinary evening routine began to console him. He moved to and fro more nimbly, preparing for the two breakfasts he would get in the morning, pouring the remains of the tea into the bottle he would carry to work with him—he had grown to enjoy cold tea—rinsing out the teapot and standing it on its head, throwing out the slops and bringing in the kindling for the morrow's fire, winding the clock and putting the cat's saucer down on a sheet of newspaper. Now, had he been by himself, he would have raked out the fire and gone off to read in bed. Instead, hospitality constrained him to say: "Have you brought a hot-water-bottle?"

She did not answer. With the kettle in one hand and the wood-basket in the other he glanced at her. Her head was resting against the back of her chair and her eyes were shut. But she was not asleep. She was openly and abjectly crying.

He built up the fire and put on the kettle. This, whatever it was about, would mean more tea. Then he patted her shoulder and said: "Poor Mary!" She put up her hand that was so plump and so demonstrably manicured and clung to his wrist. She's going to have a baby, he thought. The cat in the trap that had clawed him to the bone, clawed and clung, had been within a few days of giving birth. He had made her a nest in the woodhouse, but she had limped off to hide under a gorsebrake. The kittens had grown up and gone their wild way, and now she was pregnant again. But for poor Mary there was nothing but some sort of nursing-home.

She clung to his wrist and rubbed her head against his arm. Moulting, he thought, still clinically remembering the cat. She was going to have a baby, no doubt of it. It accounted for everything, for her nerves, for her legs, for her appetite, for her arrival. Poor Mary! Patriotism had not been enough, she had had no hatred in her heart for anybody, and so she was going to have a baby. The fortune of war. Some get killed, some get maimed, some are got with child. There ought to be a pension from the War Office. And in that dreadful uniform too, those pitiable skirts turned up. I hope to God, he thought, that I shall not have to meet the father—one of those strenuous noodles who think badly of the death sentence, like as not. I'm damned if I will. The next instant he was thinking: My poor Mary, I hope it wasn't a rape.

Meanwhile his indifferent body was complying with the schedule of his daily life, and he felt himself to be growing more and more sleepy and knew that unless he spoke he might yawn. "If you'll let go a minute, Mary, I'll make some tea."

She let go. The hand that had been so strong fell on her lap and crept into the other hand. Presently it moved again and pulled out a khaki handkerchief, and she began to mop her eyes and snort back her tears.

"This damned war! It's this damned war, Nicholas."

He groaned assentingly.

"Now that it's over, how I hate it!"

With an effort he refrained from pointing out that it was only in Europe that the war might be said to be nearly over.

"If they'd let me fight, as I wanted to, I might be killed by now. If we'd stayed in London and I'd driven an ambulance or a pump I might be killed by now. As it is, I've never been so healthy in all my life."

"You don't look well," he said. "I noticed at once that you looked tired. And you got frightfully out of breath walking up that hill."

"Fat! My healthy army fat! When I come out of the army, Nicholas, I shall come out healthy, hideous, middle-aged, and without an interest in life. And there will be hordes and hordes of me, all in the same boat. Gosh, what a crew!"

Giving up the hypothesis of a baby, he realized how much he was relinquishing. Once it was born, she would have been happy enough.

"We shall all be in that boat, dear. Besides, you're a sergeant, aren't you? That's something. You'll soon get thin, once you are out in the rough and tumble of civilian life. Once you're thin, you'll take hold, you'll get interested in something or other. Probably you'll fall in love and make a fresh start."

The kettle was boiling. He began to prepare for more tea.

"Fall in love? Fall in love?" she cried. "Not again! You see, I did it."

He paused, kettle in hand. Would nothing rid him of these turbulent kettles?

"And he was killed? I'm sorry, Mary."

"He wasn't killed. He chucked me, and now he's married to another bitch."

"And that's all?"

"And that's all."

He glanced towards the clock. It felt like midnight, but it was only half-past ten. If he could give her something stronger, some whisky, some rum. A little rum, now, in her tea. . . . But a pigeon-shooting party last week had cleared out the Red Lion of everything except aniseed cordial.

"Sugar?" he inquired.

She looked at him.

"I'm sorry. I'm sorry! I asked you that only three hours ago, didn't I? I am an insensate clod."

"That's all right, Nicholas. Actually, I never take sugar in tea. You could have had all mine, you see. Think what you've missed. Actually, why I came back was to see if you'd ever want to live with me again. Not that I thought it likely. Why should you? Anyhow, it's plain you don't. So that's over. What good tea you make!"

She drank in gulps, swallowing violently, swallowing tea and tears.

"You were always domestically inclined, weren't you? It will be a comfort to me, yes, really it will, to think of you being so happy and tidy and self-contained, with your cat and your corpse-candles and your books and your flowers. Did Robinson Crusoe have flowers on his table as well as his old cat sitting up to it like a Christian? I can't remember. Perhaps when we are both very old I may come and spend an afternoon with you on your island. And you can make me some of your nice tea and ask me if I take sugar with it. But of course I'll give you ample warning. I won't be a disquieting footprint. I did warn you this time, you know."

She had risen. She had picked up her cap and her pack and her cigarette case and her lighter and her lipstick and all her bits and pieces.

"I think I'll go to bed," she said. "I've got rather a headache."

"Yes, we'll go to bed."

Leaving the room all anyhow, he thought, as he stared at her submissive military back in the doorway. Whether it made things better, whether it made them worse, it was the only thing he could do, the only way he could comfort her. They would lie in the Wordsworthian bed, their smells of dung and of metal would mingle, her shoulder would feel like greengages and her hair would get in his mouth, and she would be silent. It was one of her graces that she was silent in bed. And afterwards, when she had gone to sleep, he would straighten himself and lie on his back, letting the day's fatigue run out of his limbs as the fleas run out of the body of a shot rabbit. And probably his last waking thought would be of the alarm-clock, poised to wake him at five-thirty, and of the limpid innocent morning in which he would go out to his work.

Time's Silvering Hand

FOR the chief part of our lives we choose our own clothes, and the choice accords with what we think or intend ourselves to be. But in old age, as in childhood, our clothes are chosen for us, and express the views, and sometimes the intentions, held about us by others. Miss Albury was dressed as her late niece, May Patcham, had thought an elderly maiden lady should be dressed: in grey, with touches of white. Under her yellow chin was a large amethyst brooch. It cast an upward reflection like a bruise. Grey, everyone knows, is softening, amethysts are Victorian. Enormously bulky, with her bruised bulldog jowl and small bloodshot eyes, Miss Albury looked like a Victorian prize-fighter long immobilized in the attitude of Whistler's mother.

But the hand which had dressed Miss Albury had not dressed the room she was sitting in. An austerer mode of domesticity was announced by the chromium-plated chairs, the bookshelves filled with works on child psychology and social research, the excellent if rather garish reproductions of modern landscape paintings with pink fields as neatly furrowed as corrugated iron roofs, avenues of blue or brown trees, red tractors approaching mauve field-factories. Only the real landscape seen through the large window, the mild clumsy contours of the west of England, corroborated Miss Albury, who might so well have retired from the ring to a quiet public-house near Exeter.

She sat, however, with her back to the window, and looked at a small electric heater near her footstool, eyeing it censoriously as though she suspected it of cheating. Even when the door opened she did not look round. During the last three weeks a great many doors had opened, front doors, back doors, bedroom doors, doors of taxis and of railway carriages; and then a new series of front doors, back doors, and bedroom doors which did not close so substantially, so assuringly, as the doors of number eleven, Spa Crescent, and which let in a moister air and a more immediate noise of household doings. For silly old May Patcham had died —what had she to die for?—and Miss Albury had been transferred from the care of a niece to the care of a cousin twice removed; and so far it was a change for the worse, since the doors did not close so well and the meals were flimsy, and Lavinia, poor little creature, had no conversation, was always in a fidget, and never seemed able to sit down.

The opening door had let in Lavinia's boy. Now, after a pause, something occurred to him. He went back to the door and carefully closed it. His clothes, too, expressed an ideal and an intention. Like Miss Albury, he was dressed in grey with touches of white. Grey shorts, grey jersey, white plimsolls. Though he was little more than a baby his clothes conscripted him into the same social order as the books and the landscape paintings.

Silently, yet in a conversational manner, he climbed on to one of the chromium-plated chairs and surveyed Miss Albury with kindness. On the whole, he liked the look of her: she was so very different to anything he had ever seen before.

"What do you think should be done about Hitler?"

After a while—it was as though she were answering him out of a deep well—she said: "About who?"

"About Hitler. Mrs. Sparrow says hanging's too good for him."

Answering out of her well Miss Albury replied: "He should be shot from a gun."

The manner of the answer pleased him. It was round and decisive, the kind of answer he craved for and did not often get. If he asked questions of Lavinia or of Miss Szuc who taught the junior class, they were apt to reply: What do *you* think, Roger? And if he said what he thought they would ask him why he thought so, and increasingly there was a hide-and-seek feeling about the conversation, as though they were watching him from behind trees. But though he approved the manner of Miss Albury's reply, he mistrusted the matter. It sounded playful.

"Timothy Senhouse saw a lady shot from a gun when

he went to the circus. But it didn't seem to hurt her and everyone clapped."

"Huh! I don't mean that sort of shooting," said Miss Albury. "Shot from a gun! That's what I said. That's what I mean. Tied to the muzzle of a gun and shot off in bits. Like the Indian Mutiny. Have you never heard of the Indian Mutiny, child?"

"I've heard of Gandhi. He's an Indian."

"Who? What? Oh yes, I know. Another of them. I'd do the same to him."

"Lavinia likes Gandhi," said the child.

"Lavinia? Who's Lavinia? She must be a great fool."

"Lavinia's my mother. She lives here, you know. But she's out just now, today's the day she works at the clinic."

No sound came from the well. Miss Albury sat with her hands folded on a white handkerchief and looked scornfully at the electric heater.

"Lavinia doesn't like Hitler, though."

A small thick tear gathered on the red rim of Miss Albury's left eye and began to slide down her cheek, pausing in the wrinkles and then hastening on. When it reached her chin it grew larger and dropped off. Nothing came of it and she did not seem to notice it.

"Mrs. Sparrow—she's the lady who comes in to help —says that one German is as bad as another, and that they ought to be finished off, the whole lot of them. They ought to be lined up, she says, and have bombs dropped on them."

He paused and inspected the old lady. She was chewing a little and perhaps thinking, but she did not speak.

"But Lavinia says . . ."

An odd appearance about Miss Albury's neck, which began to swell and redden, told him that she would not care to hear any more of what Lavinia said.

"Mrs. Sparrow has been in lots of air raids. First in London, and then in the Exeter raid. She's seen people blown to bits, just like you said. Only with bombs, you know, instead of guns. Once she tripped over something in the dark, and it was a head."

Miss Albury's head turned—so suddenly, so uncouthly, that he seemed to trip over it, just like Mrs. Sparrow.

"Have *you* been in many air raids?"

She mumbled something. She hasn't, he thought. He was pondering for a new subject—both Lavinia and Miss Szuc often enjoined tactfulness—when she said: "Go on, boy!"

"And another time she picked up a hand and it was holding a kettle, and the kettle hadn't a scratch on it. And another time she was going to a shelter, but something told her not to, and a bomb broke the sewer and they were all drowned before anyone could do anything. And another time she was going to a shelter—another shelter—and just as she turned the corner she heard something coming up the street like children coming out of school. And she shone her torch on it, and it was rats, hundreds and hundreds of rats, all screaming because they were singed and burned."

At school there was a pig, and sometimes during Nature Study they scratched it. Miss Albury was now looking exactly like the pig when scratched: as pink, as subsiding, as helplessly delighted. She was grunting too.

"Mrs. Sparrow said she could smell the smell of roast meat as they went past," he added.

Mrs. Sparrow had said nothing of the sort. He had felt that she should have done so, and had added this confirming detail to his private registration of her narrative. Of course there would have been a smell of roast meat, roast rat, and only Mrs. Sparrow's adenoids had stood between her and it. But now, spoken out loud, it did not sound like Mrs. Sparrow. Entangled in the solicitude of the creative artist, he frowned and fell silent.

"Go on, boy! Go on! Tell me some more."

The pig, though at times becoming rather confusing, always remained lovable. Miss Albury had suddenly ceased to be lovable. She was growing purple all over, as though the reflection of her brooch had turned into a kind of unpleasant sunrise and was suffusing her. Even beneath the grey and white, he thought, she was turning purple. And it was horrible.

"Ever so many old ladies were burned to death!"

The doors of the house, so washably painted, so sensibly contrived not to harbour dust, were nevertheless, as Miss Albury had observed, thin and ill-fitting. And so when Lavinia let herself in she could hear not only Mrs. Sparrow rattling the luncheon trays in the kitchen, but Roger talking in the sitting-room. He was saying something about old ladies too, and his voice was over-excited. What a mercy that she had decided to sacrifice her midday break to coming home to see whether everything was all right.

Slender, anxious, large-eyed, looking like a careworn kitten, she entered the room. Her lips smiled, her eyes surveyed. Neither of them spoke.

"I thought I'd just run back for a minute to see that you were comfortable. I hope you are not giving Cousin Mildred your cold, darling? Perhaps she doesn't want you in here?"

"Not at all, not at all." Out of her massive repose—and somehow she now looked larger than ever—Miss Albury spoke graciously, and smiled, and smoothed her hands together. "We have been having quite a little chat. And your litle boy has been telling me some very interesting things. Ve–ry, ve–ry in–ter–esting. *Must* you open the window, dear?"

Lavinia murmured something about germs, and only for a minute. At the inrush of fresh air the boy shook himself, looked round, and began to sneeze, like an animal awaking.

A Pigeon

THE two large windows of the room on the first floor looked straight out into the trees of Lincoln's Inn Fields. A pigeon was cooing among the greenery. Tears rushed into Irene's eyes. She had a sentimental character, and how sad it was, really, a girl of her age, as innocent as that bird, and all by herself, sitting opposite a solicitor called Mr. Winander and having an interview about her divorce.

When she had wiped her eyes their gaze returned to Mr. Winander.

Mr. Winander was looking at his notes. He was by no means her idea of a solicitor. He was more like a violinist, for his hair was long and his eyes were cavernous, and he was thin and swarthy. On the wall behind him hung an oil painting, and that, too, was swarthy and cavernous, an old master. Something was going on in its dusky recesses, and a halo floated above the head of the principal character. Teresa, who had spoken so highly of Mr. Winander from personal experience, had not mentioned that he was a religious man. She had said that he was a gentleman all over and yet you felt he was a real man of the world.

Looking up from his notes Mr. Winander said:

"Well, Mrs. Johnston, as far as I can see there is nothing here likely to worry us. No children, an undefended case. It all seems quite straightforward. Do you smoke?"

When he had lit her cigarette he pushed forward across the wide table the largest ash-tray she had ever set eyes on. It was like a glass cocktail-tray, and so shiny that it seemed almost an outrage to drop ash in it.

"But I must warn you, it will take time, we may have to wait a long time for a hearing. There are so many divorce cases on the list. The Courts can't keep up with them."

"Dreadful, isn't it?"

"Queues everywhere," said Mr. Winander soothingly.

There was a label on the frame of the oil painting, and now that she had seen it and read it she could perceive quite clearly that the picture represented Jesus Suffering the Little Ones to Come unto Him. She had nothing against that kind of religion.

"Mrs. Johnston, you must forgive me asking this. Are you quite sure that you wish to go forward with a divorce?"

"Oh yes, definitely. I never was one to stay where I wasn't welcome."

"Quite so, quite so."

"It isn't that I'm narrow-minded, you know," said Mrs. Johnston with earnestness, "or that I don't know what men are. I could have put up with that, in reason. Hugh's very attractive, and only human, when all's said and done. But to be looked at as if you weren't there, or as if you were something that had got in by accident—you can't really call that a marriage."

"No," said Mr. Winander, and made another note.

Never before had anyone made notes of what she said. It was quite an experience, it made her feel as if she were giving an interview for the papers. "It's somehow so devastating to feel that you are nothing to a man."

He did not, however, make a note of this, but offered her another cigarette. His hands were clean as only a man's hands can be. They were even cleaner than Hugh's, and God knows he made enough fuss about them, screaming out loud if he found as much as a hair on the soap. But Mr. Winander would never scream out loud. He was not that kind of man, you could tell that at a glance. He was full of self-control, and rather reserved. Of course, seeing so much of the murky side of life must have made him disillusioned; and that was why, though he was so much like a violinist, you could see he was not really a violinist. But it was only on the surface he was disillusioned. Teresa had not fathomed him. Teresa never had had much feeling for intuition.

"You understand, Mrs. Johnston, that between serving the divorce papers and the case coming up for hearing you must not go back to Mr. Johnston?"

"I shouldn't think of it," she said. "He doesn't want me."

Smiling at her and looking even more as if he might suffer little ones, Mr. Winander went on: "And that if you should meet anyone else who does want you, Mrs. Johnston, you must do nothing about it until your decree nisi is through."

And, forsaking all others, keep thee only unto him. . . . There was something about Mr. Winander's voice and the way he addressed her from beyond his desk—an expanse so far-reaching that even his enormous ash-tray was but an incident on it—which made her feel as though she were being married in a church.

"Oh no, Mr. Winander, I wouldn't think of that either, I assure you. I'm not that sort of person at all."

"I always tell my clients—my divorce clients—that getting a divorce is like hatching an egg. It entails a rather tiresome interval of leading a dull quiet life."

Gazing at him with her beautiful eyes Mrs. Johnston remarked sadly: "I dare say it may surprise you, but I have never really known what love means—not actually."

"Before you go"—Mr. Winander touched his table bell—"I want you to meet Mr. Upjohn. Mr. Upjohn is my head clerk. He is, I might say, my second self. I am going to ask him . . ."

The door opened and Mr. Winander's second self appeared so instantaneously that he might have been waiting just behind it. He was a short stocky man with a red face, and he wore eyeglasses.

"Mrs. Johnston, may I introduce Mr. Upjohn? Mr.

Upjohn, this is Mrs. Hugh Johnston, a new client. I want you to take particular care of her case."

They were all on their feet. "How d'you do," said Mr. Upjohn in a quite common voice. "Excuse me, I think you've dropped your gloves. You mustn't go away without them, you know. That would never do."

And as though he were already beginning to take particular care of her case, he bobbed down for the gloves and bobbed up again, presenting them to her with a little bristling bow.

Beyond the tall windows the plane tree serenely waved its branches, but the pigeon had left off cooing.

The Cold

THE Cold came into the household by Mrs. Ryder. At first she said she had picked it up at the Mothers' Union Meeting; later—it was the kind of cold that gets worse with time—she attributed it to getting chilled through waiting in the village shop while that horrible Beryl Legg took over half an hour to decide whether she would spend her points on salmon or Spam. Never a thought for her child, of course, who by now should be getting prunes and cereals. Whoever the father might be, one would have expected the girl to show some maternal feeling—but no!

The next person to get The Cold was old Mr. Ryder, the Rector's father, and he immediately gave it to old Mrs. Ryder. They did not have it so badly, but at their age and after all they had gone through in London before they could make up their minds to evacuate themselves to their son's country parish one had to put them to bed with trays, just to be on the safe side. Dry and skinny, they lay in the spare-room twin beds like two recumbent effigies on tombs, and chattered to each other in faded high-pitched voices. Segregated from the normal family life, they had re-established that rather tiresome specialness which sometimes made it difficult to realize that they were really dear Gerald's parents. It is very nice to be cultivated, of course, but somehow in war time it does jar to labour upstairs with a heavy supper-tray and hear, beyond the door, two animated voices discussing Savonarola; and then to hear the voices silenced, like mice when one throws a shoe in their direction, as one knocked on the door and called out brightly, "Supper, darlings!"; and to know, as clearly as if one had seen it, that old Mrs. Ryder was stubbing out one of her cigarettes. That jarred too, especially as she smoked such very heavy ones.

From the old Ryders The Cold descended to the third and fourth generations, to Geraldine and her two boys. Thence it leaped upon the Rector. Leaped was indeed the word. He had set out for the funeral looking the picture of health; he returned haggard and shivering, and so terribly depressed that she had said to herself: "Influenza!" But it was only The Cold, The Cold in its direst form.

"*No!*" exclaimed Mrs. Allingham, indefatigable secretary of the Women's Institute. "*Not* the Rector?"

"If you had been in church on Sunday you wouldn't need to ask."

The indefatigable secretary was a matter for regret on Sundays, when she was more often seen taking her terriers over the common than herself to Saint Botolph and All Angels. Such a pity!—for in every other way she was an excellent influence.

Recovering herself rather too easily, for it showed

that such recoveries were nothing to the rebuked one, Mrs. Allingham went on: "All seven of you! For I can see you've got it too. You poor things! My dear, what do you do about handkerchiefs, now that the laundry collects only once a fortnight? Can I lend you some?"

"Stella washes them."

"Your marvellous Stella! What would you do without her? I hope she is still standing up."

"I can't imagine Stella failing us," said Mrs. Ryder with satisfaction.

In the sixth autumn of the war Mrs. Ryder was a little tired. She was feeling her age. Her last tailor-made was definitely not quite a success and, say what you will, people do judge one by appearances. She could not help noticing that strangers were not as respectful as they might be, though, no doubt, the unhelpfulness of Utility corsets played its part in the decline of manners. In the parish, too, there was much to grieve the Rector and the Rector's wife. The old simple natural order of things was upset by all these changes: the grocer's son actually a Captain, as much a Captain (and indeed senior in captaincy) as dear Geraldine's Neville; the butcher's wife in Persian lamb; the resolutions at the Parish Council only to be described as Communist; and the girls, her own Girls' Club girls, behaving so shockingly that she often wondered what the mothers of these poor American soldiers would think if they only knew what their sons were exposed to. But she had Stella. And having Stella she had all things.

No one could pick holes in Stella. There were no holes to pick. Stella was physically perfect, not deaf, nor halt, nor imbecile. Stella did not wear glasses and did wear a cap and apron. Stella was functionally perfect: she did not dawdle, she did not waste, she did not gossip, she was clean, punctual, reliable, she was always cheerful and willing, she scrubbed her own back-kitchen and mended the choir surplices; and though, of course, her wages were perfectly adequate, no one could say that the Ryders bribed her to stay with them—Stella stayed through devotion, she could have got twice as much elsewhere. Finally, Stella was a good girl. In a time when manners and morality had gone down alike before expediency, when householders snatched at trousered and cigarette-smoking evacuees if the evacuee would "help with light domestic duties," when even the houses that ought to set an example employed girls with illegitimate babies and glossed over the capitulation with pretexts of being compassionate and broad-minded, Mrs. Ryder continued to boast the ownership of a virgin, a strong womanly virgin, who wore skirts, fastened up unwaved hair in a sensible knob, and said, "Yes, ma'am."

Naturally, one took care of such a treasure. Stella's cold was given quite as much consideration as any other family cold and dosed out of the same bottle. In the worst of the epidemic Mrs. Ryder said that if Stella did not feel better by midday she really must be sent to bed. For several evenings Mrs. Ryder and Geraldine washed up the supper dishes so that Stella might sit quietly by the stove with the surplices instead of shivering in the back kitchen. And when Stella's cough persisted after the other coughs had died away, Geraldine went in specially by bus to look for black-currant lozenges and came back with some wonderful pastilles flavoured with horehound.

But it was a long time before Stella's cough could be distinguished from the other coughs by outlasting them. The Cold was such a treacherous type of cold. When you thought you'd got rid of it, it came back. Like beggars, said old Mrs. Ryder (for they were downstairs again, one could not keep them in bed indefinitely). Like dandelions, said her son. Geraldine said that she believed it was nutritional. Of course, one ought not to complain, the food was marvellous really, more marvellous than ever if one thought about poor old Europe; but still, it wasn't the same, was it? She had met Mrs. Allingham, and Mrs. Allingham had inquired, of course, about The Cold, and had said that in 1918 everyone had just the same kind of cold, it was quite remarkable. What did the Grand-Grands say? Did they have colds in 1918?

"We had much better rum, and more of it," said old Mrs. Ryder. She looked at her husband very affectionately, he stroked his beard and looked back at her, and so they both avoided seeing Mrs. Ryder catch her breath like one who holds back a justified reproach because experience has shown that reproaches are vain. The Rector, even more imperceptive, remarked that it was very kind of his parents to make poor Stella a nightcap, he hoped it would do her good. He had seen rum do a lot of good when he was a chaplain in Flanders. Stella was a good girl, a very good girl. They would be badly off without her.

For some reason Mrs. Ryder and her daughter now began discussing how tomorrow they really must polish the stair-rods and the bathroom taps. They would make time for it somehow if Mrs. Ryder did the altar vases before breakfast and Stella took the boys with her when she went to the farm for milk. If the boys wore their rubber boots the slush wouldn't do them any harm.

John was five, Michael was three. You couldn't really call them spoilt, they were just war-time, lacking the influence of a father about the house. But not spoilt. Besides, Geraldine liked boys to behave as boys; it would be too awful if they grew up like Neville's ghastly young brother who would sit for hours stroking the cat and turn off the wireless whenever it became worth listening to. A dressing-room had been made over as their playroom, but it was pretty bleak up there and naturally they preferred the kitchen. If anyone spoilt them it was Stella, who didn't seem able to say no to them. And if they were rather fretful just now it wasn't to be wondered at, it was The Cold.

The doctor's sister, a rather uncongenial character

with independent means, used to refer to Mrs. Ryder and her daughter as Bright and Breezy. They had a great deal in common, she said, but Geraldine had more of it, and was Breezy. Geraldine now had more of The Cold. Her sneezes were louder, her breathing more impeded, her nose redder, and her handkerchiefs more saturated. Throughout The Cold Mrs. Ryder had kept on her feet: as a daughter-in-law, mother, grandmother, and wife to a Rector, she could not do otherwise; but Geraldine had not merely kept on her feet, she stamped and trampled. She scorned precautions, she went everywhere and kissed everybody, just as usual. She did not believe, not she! in cosseting a cold. What are colds? Everyone has them, they are part of English life. Foreigners have things with spots, the English have colds. She made having a cold seem part of the national tradition like playing cricket and Standing Alone.

And so, when they had all got rid of The Cold and even Stella only coughed at night, Geraldine seemed to be breaking the Union Jack at the mast-head when she woke the echoes of the kitchen with a violent sneeze and asserted: "I'm beginning another cold. And what's more, I can tell it's going to be a snorter. So watch out, one and all!"

"I do hope not, Miss Geraldine," answered Stella.

It was rather touching the way Stella still called her Miss Geraldine—as if to Stella the passage of time were nothing, a tide that flowed past the kitchen threshold but never wetted her feet.

"No jolly hope!"

Geraldine went out. Presently she could be heard telling her mother about the new cold. Mrs. Ryder sounded unenthusiastic, she said she only hoped it would not last so long this time, as otherwise it would spoil Christmas. Stella went on rubbing stale bread through a sieve for the war-time Christmas pudding. It needed a lot of breadcrumbs, in fact, you might as well call it bread-pudding and be done with it, but Mrs. Ryder said the children must be brought up to love Christmas. They stood on either side of the table, rolling bread-pills and throwing them at each other.

The recipe for the war-time Christmas pudding which needed a lot of breadcrumbs also called for grated carrot. When she had finished the breadcrumbs and put them on a high shelf where she hoped the children might not get at them, Stella went into the back kitchen and began to clean carrots over the sink. If you rub stale bread through a fine sieve for any length of time you are apt to develop a pain between the shoulders. She had such a pain; and the change of climate from the kitchen, which was hot, to the back kitchen, which was cold, made her more conscious of it. When she had cleaned the carrots she went back to the kitchen. The two little boys were still there and Mrs. Ryder had been added.

"Oh, Stella, I came in to say that I thought we would have onion soup tonight, as well as the fishcakes. Mrs. Hartley thinks she has another cold coming on."

"Yes, ma'am. I wish to . . ."

Mrs. Ryder swept on. "And, Stella, of course I know how busy you are, but all the same I think it would be better *not* to leave the babies alone in here. When I came in I found John playing with the flat-irons. Of course they were cold, but they might have been hot. Perhaps a little more thoughtfulness . . . With such young children one cannot be too thoughtful."

"Very well, ma'am. But I wish to leave, ma'am."

"Beddy-bies, beddy-bies!" exclaimed Mrs. Ryder. "Come now, John, come, Michael! Kiss dear Stella good night, and off with you to your little beds. Now a nice kiss . . ."

"Don't want to," said the child.

Mrs. Ryder seized a child under either arm, waved them in the direction of Stella's face, and conveyed them out of the room, shutting the door on them with a firm, sweet "God bless you, my babies!" Then, flushed with exertion, with difficulty withstanding the impulse to go with them, she turned back, hoping that her ears had deceived her and knowing too well that they hadn't.

"I wish to leave, ma'am."

"Stella! What do you mean?"

"I wish to leave, ma'am."

There she stood, grating carrots as if the children's Christmas were nothing to her.

"But, Stella . . . I *trusted* you! After all these years! Why, we all look on you as a friend. What has happened to you?"

Could it be, could it be? Stella was short and the kitchen table was high and anything may be happening behind an apron. In a convulsion of the imagination Mrs. Ryder rehearsed herself saying that one should not penalize a poor girl for a solitary slip, that kindness, a good home, the example of a Christian home-life which means so much, etc., etc. A harlot hope raised its head, and at the same moment she heard Stella say quite idiotically:

"I think I'm catching another cold."

"Good heavens, girl, is that a reason for going? I've never heard such nonsense!"

"It's nothing but one cold after another. Cold, cold, cold! Work, work, work! It's not a fit place for me. Both my aunties were chesty, and if I stay here I shall go the same way, I know it. What's more, I'm going tomorrow. I don't mind about my money, I'm going tomorrow. I want to get away while I've still got the strength."

"In war time," said Mrs. Ryder in her sternest Mothers' Union manner, the manner unfurled only for urgent things like War Savings Rallies and Blood Transfusion Drives, "in war time, when our boys are shedding their blood without a moment's hesitation . . . and you are positively running away from a simple cold in the head. I cannot believe it!"

Without a spark of incredulity she banged the door behind her.

There was the Rectory hall. There were the coats

and the hats and the children's rubber boots and the umbrellas, and the brass letter-tray, and the copper gong, and the stair-rods ascending. There was Gerald writing in his study, and Geraldine gargling in the bathroom, and in the sitting-room the two old Ryders chattering like love-birds. Here was her home, her dear (except for the old Ryders), her dear, dear home, where everything spoke of love and loving labour; the happy busy home that was—Mrs. Allingham's own words—a beacon to the parish.

But now . . .

Not Stella? Not your marvellous Stella?

The words seemed to dart at her from every side, stabbing through the unsuccessful tailor-made into her ageing flesh. Tomorrow the Sewing Circle met at the Rectory. Only self-respect withheld her from running back into the kitchen to throw herself on Stella's mercy, to beg, on her knees even to beg and implore that Stella would change her mind, would stay, would at any rate stay to see them over Christmas. Self-respect was rage and fury. Presently they died down. But she remained in the hall, knowing that any appeal to Stella would be in vain.

Tomorrow the Sewing Circle met. They met at three in the afternoon. Stella would be out of the house before then. *She must be!* Mrs. Ryder thanked God that self-respect had stood like an angel between her and a fatal false step. "Stella has gone. Poor Stella! I could not keep her." A few such words, and a grave grieved silence, nothing that was not true, strictly true; and the Sewing Circle might draw its own conclusions. Cooking, sweeping, scrubbing, doing everything that for so long Stella had done, she could still hold up her head.

View Halloo

ONE of the amenities of the house called Gwenddwr—not so striking as the waterfall, which the house-agent had particularized as "unusually unique," nor so practical as the gooseberry bushes, but still an amenity—was that it had a telephone. The line went to the post-office at Dolwen-goch, and thence you depended on Mrs. Lloyd for calls to the butcher, the baker, the doctor, or London. As they were all Londoners, the calls to London were frequent. In order to keep things on a business footing among the seven people sharing Gwenddwr as a holiday dwelling, Antoinette Kauffman had put a note-book by the telephone.

Now while Mrs. Lloyd was managing her call to the butcher, she looked idly through it. Naturally it contained more than records of phone calls—such books always do. There were anchors and vine-leaves and blackamoors, there were notes of train-times and phone numbers, drafts of telegrams and fragmentary records of conversations. There were scraps of loose paper too, and on a sudden puff of wind through the gaspingly open window one of these whirled to the floor. Picking it up she saw a drawing. It was the outline of a woman's head and shoulders with a jagged line transfixing the head from above. Underneath was written: *Lightning striking Mrs. Lawther.*

The line clicked. Mrs. Lloyd remarked: "There's no answer from Mr. Jones, Mrs. Kauffman. No wonder, he's slaughtering. But I have a telegram for Limbo."

The word seemed to be Limbo. "But none of us is called Limbo."

"It's from London," said Mrs. Lloyd. "Wait you now till my hand is upon it."

Antoinette looked again at *Lightning striking Mrs. Lawther* and thought that if it had been by Matisse it would have been very characteristic. But who was it by? She did not recognize the handwriting. Even after a fortnight of sharing Gwenddwr it discomposed her to be living with people whose handwritings she did not know. But probably it was one of the children.

"Here we are, Mrs. Kauffman. Handed in at Paddington, London, August thirteenth, at eleven-thirty, to Mainwaring, Gwenddwr, Dolwen-goch, Merioneth —'Can you do short feature supernatural by Friday Jumbo.' "

In order to take it down she had to shut the window. The moment the window was shut the smell of Gwenddwr took over from the noise of the waterfall. The smell of Gwenddwr was the smell of a boiled family Bible—which was the more unaccountable as Gwenddwr was such a completely agnostic house. Everything about it was agnostic: its enormous plate-glass windows, its square rooms lit by remorselessly central and unshaded lights of high wattage, its furnishings, which were inflexibly suites, and the fact that in a landscape of slate and stone it was built of red brick. With the waterfall flashing beside it in a gulley choked with ferns, and embowered in hydrangeas and fuchsias, it stood there like a protest against Welsh spelling and the Arthurian Legend.

Restoring *Lightning striking Mrs. Lawther* to the note-book, Antoinette went in search of Miss Mainwaring.

"Why can't these editors leave one alone?" inquired Iris Mainwaring with natural pride. "Just because I once wrote a piece about werewolves! Well, I suppose I shall never hear the last of it."

"I did a lobster Armoricaine once."

"Really?" After a pitying pause Miss Mainwaring continued: "Does that help? Shall I write about a lobster that turned blue at a dinner-party?"

"Write a story about a horrible woman who wore fur."

Antoinette had supposed that the children were in the garden among the advantageous gooseberry bushes. There were three children in the party, the Tupmans' Judith and the Hepburns' boys, William and Francis. This was Francis. He rose up from behind the sofa and began to scratch his leg in an inspired manner.

"She wore fur. And ear-rings. And a great deal of beastly expensive scent. And stockings. And she thought everyone bowed down to her."

"I see. A Left story. Do go on, Francis!"

"And one day she went up on a mountain in her fur coat. And a bear saw her. It was a he bear and it thought she was its female. So it chased her all over the mountain till she climbed a tree. The tree broke and she fell off into a waterfall and was drowned."

"It's a charming story. But it's not supernatural. No ghosts in it, you know."

"Oh yes, it is. Her ghost had to stay in the waterfall, howling with cold, and ever since people have heard her teeth chattering all night. It's called 'The Haunted Waterfall.' "

"What became of the bear?" Antoinette asked.

"The bear was all right."

Suddenly losing interest he walked away. Iris Mainwaring began to look preoccupied, so Antoinette also left the room, pausing only to take some dead meadowsweet out of a vase. That is the worst of wild flowers. Children will bring them in, one puts them in water from compassion, and three hours later they are dead.

Children also bring in woolly-bear caterpillars, frogs, sticklebats in jampots, large stones, old and verminous birds' nests, interesting sticks, dead slow-worms for purposes of investigation, gifted kittens, and half-chewed crab-apples. It is natural, and she would not have minded if it had not fretted Leonard, who was by nature neat. Leonard was also by nature kind, but ten years' doctoring in a slum neighbourhood had left their mark. This was his first holiday since 1940; and because it had been her idea to cover the expense of a trout-stream by sharing Gwenddwr, and because she had put the advertisement in *The New Statesman* and selected the Hepburns, the Tupmans, and Miss Mainwaring from the many who answered it, she felt as anxious as a hen.

Yet Leonard loved children. The gifts he heaped upon her, the marmot coat, the pearls, the black-marketed eau-de-cologne, all so extravagantly beyond their means and above their station, carried, she knew, a desperate assurance that her sterility, her persistent nymph-like slenderness, had not qualified his devotion. If William and Francis had been more like Judith, or if the parental Hepburns had shown a trifle more parental solicitude . . . As it was, they were out all day rock-climbing, and the only solicitude displayed was Bridget Hepburn's anxiety lest William and Francis should become inhibited or constipated. But inhibition was worse, God forbid they should become enslaved to regular habits!

The Tupmans, too, were out all day. Mary Tupman fished silently, and Captain Tupman looked for wild-flowers with his one eye. The Tupmans were her best pick. They were gentle and polite. Unfortunately they were both almost incapable of speech, and this had given Leonard the idea that they thought they were not getting their money's worth.

The noise of Miss Mainwaring's typewriter was now added to the fatalistic roar of the waterfall. There was no fatalism about the typewriter. It went in fits and starts and conveyed creative pettishness. Then there was an exclamation of annoyance, the squawk of a chair pushed back. Footsteps approached the door, the door was firmly shut. Antoinette desisted from trying to tidy the hall, took a basket and went out. She would walk down to where Leonard was fishing, and perhaps get some blackberries or some mushrooms on the way. She was one of those women who cannot go upstairs or down, indoors or out, empty-handed.

Outside the house the beauty of the landscape fell on her like an admonition. Under the cuckoo-coloured sky the wet green of the ferns and the wet black of the rocks was like a Chinese brocade. Everything was innocent, heartless, wildly and inconceivably at peace. She twisted off a bracken-frond to wave at the flies and began to walk down the valley. She had gone some way when it occurred to her that as an insurance against any visitations of conscience she would be well advised to give a last glance to those children. She turned back. They were not in the garden, nor in the paddock, nor among the hazels, nor was there a body in the pool under the waterfall. She began to feel herself growing hot, panicked, and angry. How red Gwenddwr looked, and how rectangular!—redder than ever now, because the sky was darkening for another of those mountain thunder-storms. *Lightning striking Mrs. Lawther.*

"Mad Bulls tossing Mrs. Lawther. There you are!"

It was as though her thought had pulled the words

out of the air. They came, however, from the wood-shed.

"I want to draw a bull too. William, I want to draw a bull."

"You can't. Not on this. It would spoil the magic. Draw a bull in your own book if you want to."

"Well, lend me the pencil."

"That would spoil the magic too. Go and get a pencil for yourself, there are always pencils by the telephone."

So that was what became of her pencils.

"But don't go yet! You can't get out of the magic circle till it's all finished. Now, Judith, give me three of your hairs. And pull them out properly, mind, so that it hurts. No cheating!"

Judith giggled, and exclaimed *Ow!* Then a match was struck.

"Now! All together! Hateful Mrs. Lawther! Hateful Mrs. Lawther! Mad Bulls tossing Hateful Mrs. Lawther!"

The stamping and the chanting ended as efficiently as a drill, and were followed by a religious silence.

So that was what happened to the matches too. But who was Mrs. Lawther? And was this how uninhibited children played?

Apparently Judith was less uninhibited than the Hepburns, for now she said in an infidel, dissatisfied voice: "But I still don't understand why we have to call her Mrs. Lawther. Why can't we just say Mrs.—"

"Ssh! We must never say it. That's another part of the magic. Besides, Lawther is just what she's like. Law–ther, Law–ther. All dragged-out and slimy."

"My turn now," said Francis. "I've thought of a beauty. Red Rats eating Mrs. Lawther. I shall do it with a red pencil. I saw one on Leonard's desk."

He came prancing out of the woodshed. Seeing her he stopped dead, and opened his mouth as if about to scream.

"It's all right," she said. "It's only me. I'm going to pick blackberries. But if any of you want anything, Miss Mainwaring's indoors."

He wrenched his mouth into a false, beaming smile and ran off as fast as his legs could carry him. From within the woodshed there came no sound.

All encounters with children are touched with social embarrassment. Antoinette was sorry she had overheard this private performance. It had shocked her. It seemed false and old-fashioned, as though these children were playing at being the children in a children's book of an earlier generation. A day or so before when Lionel Hepburn was explaining the atomic bomb in scornful popular language William and Francis were not only able to understand him, but alone among his listeners were genuinely and impersonally interested. Then she had said to herself that after all the future would be in the hands of children brought up to face the truth with tranquillity. Yet here they were playing at sympathetic magic and secret societies like a little Ku Klux Klan. She waved her fern frond violently and looked about for something to distract her.

By the time she saw the tip of Leonard's rod flicking among the hazels she had filled her basket with mushrooms. She waited till he saw her and clambered up the bank to where she sat.

"Any luck, darling?" she said, her mind on the morrow's breakfast.

"All the luck in the world, my pet, since you've come out to meet me."

He scrubbed his hand on the grass and then patted her cheek. She thought with a pang that it was quite true. He loved her like that. But absorbed in his welfare or his comfort she forgot his pleasure. A world of care stood between them, they could meet only for an instant, like prisoners meeting in an exercise yard.

He saw her glance wander towards his creel. "Four," he said.

"Splendid! With the mushrooms, and Mary Tupman is sure to have caught something, that's breakfast. It's lucky we are such good providers, you and I, Salmon and Gluckstein. I should hate to breakfast off the Hepburns' fossils garnished with Captain Tupman's parsley fern."

"I wish you did not have to slave for these people."

She shrugged her shoulders. "It's all right," she said. "I do it very well."

"Sufferance is the badge of all our tribe." His

face contracted, he stared into the water, stiffly trembling. She laid her hand on his hand and waited till she felt it relax.

"I rather wish I had not chosen them all Christians," she said. "Sometimes I think Gwenddwr is one of my mistakes."

"They're usually out on their crusades, we only see them at meals. Just now I think Gwenddwr is paradise."

They sat in paradise, smoking to keep off the midges, till the dusk brimmed up the valley and the red of the rowan berries had darkened like drying blood and was almost black. It was Leonard who got up to go.

The red of Gwenddwr had also darkened. Lights glared from its windows, and through the noise of the waterfall came the clatter of Iris Mainwaring composing something supernatural for Jumbo.

"Where are the children, Antoinette? It's time they were indoors. That little Judith is not strong. This morning she had rings round her eyes. I should worry about her if she were mine."

He stood in the garden, calling and whistling. There was no answer.

"I expect they are indoors, helping Minnie to get supper. This is the evening she comes up, you know. They like her."

They entered the house and instantly Iris Mainwaring appeared.

"Oh, *here* you are, Antoinette! I wondered where

you had got to. The phone's been ringing and ringing."

"I am so sorry."

"What was it?" Leonard asked. Already he was looking at the mess in the hall.

"I really can't remember. Something about no sausages. Anyhow, I made a note of it. Everybody's in, by the way."

"Oh well, that's good," said Leonard. "And how have you been getting on, Iris? You should write a piece about the waterfall. How quiet everyone is tonight, eh? Where are the children?"

"Still gorging gooseberries."

"But we came up through the garden and I called them and no one answered."

Iris Mainwaring did not answer either.

Antoinette said: "I'll go and see about the message. Come, Leonard." For the telephone was on the first floor landing, and a timely pretext for removing him from any further inspection of that mess.

Only now, cast out of paradise, did she remember that Francis had been going to take Leonard's red pencil. Upstairs the smell of boiled Bible was stronger than ever. Sword-blades of violent light prodded from around bedroom doors, and someone was having a bath. Mr. Jones had no sausages. It was improbable that Leonard would choose this moment to want his red pencil, but to be on the safe side she carried the drawing of *Lightning striking Mrs. Lawther* along to their bedroom. Leonard was interested in children's drawings, he had helped to organize an International Exhibition of Child Art.

"Look what I found in the telephone book. Isn't it like a Matisse?"

He looked at it and the blood darkened his face and he began to tremble with fury.

"Intolerable insolence!"

"But why? What's wrong with it?"

"Why? Why? What's wrong with it? Look for yourself, Antoinette, and don't be silly."

She looked again at the outlined head on the long neck and the zigzag of lightning transfixing it.

"Do you mean it's that Blackshirt thing, the Flash in the Pan? But I'm sure it's not that. It's just how every child draws lightning."

"Can't you see that it is *you?* The lightning is nothing. But this is a caricature of you."

There was no cover in the room so bleakly lit till she pulled out her hairpins and began to comb her long black hair over her face. She combed and combed, and it seemed to her that she was combing the waterfall, and no waterfall could flow more icily than the cold shivers running up and down her back.

"Children are silly," she said at last. "It doesn't mean anything, Leonard."

Parting her hair she looked into the mirror to see him. He was still sitting on the bed, his back was towards her, and he was smoothing out the sheet of paper which in his wrath he had crumpled into a ball.

"But there's talent in it, you know. Oh yes, there's talent."

His sigh seemed to fill the room, to fill the world.

She began to brush the sweet-scented oil into her hair. There was still the red pencil to be got over; but the rest, with luck, she could keep to herself. And what was it, after all, to make an outcry about? What was one Jew more or less among the millions, the millions? And barren, at that. She looked again at Leonard in the mirror. He was growing much balder, he was, in fact, bald. The smooth dome rising above the ring of grizzled curls was sun-burned, and probably he should not go out without a hat. His tweeds neither fitted him nor suited him. They were correct, well-cut, very expensive, decently worn; and they sat on him and denounced his nationality. Even now Leonard had not learned not to wear English clothes, make English jokes, behave among English people as if there were no difference between him and them. It was his proudest, vainest boast that he was English, and free, in a free country. He was as trustful as a child, as obstinate as a mule. How could she get him away in time? And where?

English Climate

As GUNNER BROCK opened the door of the recreation hut a volley of rain came in, and a cat. He shut the door and turned to look at the cat. It was a new ginger, he noted. Cats came and went on the anti-aircraft site, and this annoyed Gunner Brock, who had a tidy mind and felt that cats should be permanent. One grievance flicked him into voicing another. "Perhaps you'll have got those books changed by the time I'm back," he said to Gunner Ives, who was sunk deep in a chair, reading.

A dozen exhausted volumes sagged on a shelf by the door. Their subject matter did not so much express the eclecticism of the Welfare Officer who had brought them out from the library a fortnight earlier, as the fact that he had chosen them after lunching with a friend.

"Not till I've finished *The Wide Wide World,*" said Gunner Ives, who was a Marxist. "Just listen to this . . ."

Gunner Brock fidgeted on one foot and then the other and finally interrupted him. "I've got to catch my train," he said.

"Well," Gunner Ives said, his glance still drawn irresistibly towards the paragraph he had been reading, "so long. Have a good leave."

"Thanks," Brock said, and went out into the rain.

It was a five-mile walk to the station and the last mile and a half he hurried, but he needn't have done so: the afternoon train was twenty minutes late. He found a seat and began his journey of nineteen hours and five changes. The railway track ran within half a mile of the anti-aircraft site. Through the streaming window he saw briefly the huts, the smoke from the cookhouse chimney, the searchlight and the locator in their canvas hoods. It looked as though some demented fair had set itself up on the heath and now waited for the arrival of customers.

By midday tomorrow he would be home. At midday tomorrow it would still be raining. He would spend the afternoon having a bath, wallowing at full length, hearing the chirp of rain in the gutters and the gentle wallop of the bath water running down the overflow pipe. There he would lie, reading. And downstairs would be Mother, rattling the tea things, Edna coming home from her office, then Dad. At seven Mother and Edna would go off to the Y.M.C.A. canteen, splashing so bravely through the wet. How on earth did women support life when there wasn't a war? What would Mother do when this war was over and the canteen was closed and she was left with but one son (if that, indeed) instead of those dozens of "my boys," towards all of whom she felt like a mother? A retired colonel, however fire-eating, takes up gardening or plays golf or bridge or busies himself with local administration or rings migratory birds, for men are flippant, variable, easily amused. But to a woman's iron energies what appeasement can peace bring?

Left to themselves he and Dad would wash up and get supper. The cat, the fixed and proper family cat, would rub around their legs. Once again he would feel that profound sensation of being indoors—a far more intimate sensation than that of merely being at home. Gradually he would adjust himself to small rooms, unechoing floors, passages, stairways, the complexity of a house. And upstairs his bedroom, close-fitting as a thimble, would wait for him. Silently, privately, intensely, it would await the moment when he switched on the bedside lamp and shut the door after him. In that room he would slowly and luxuriously undress, and luxuriously slide between the sheets and find the hot-water bottle, and lie for a breathing space listening to the rain, summoning his senses for that journey of the hand to the bookshelf. Which should it be? The fourth from the left was Boswell's *Life*, then the even ranks of the Fitzgerald *Letters*. In his fingers stirred a consciousness of how that bookshelf would feel: the orderly row, the smooth backs, the sharp corners—a world away from that heap of flaccid derelicts by the door of the recreation hut.

Waking at a burst of light and cold morning air as three schoolboys, smelling freshly of soap and early rising, climbed in over his legs, Gunner Brock saw that the weather had cleared. The sun was rising into a sky full of wind and movement. Presently he changed into the last of his trains. It was a stopping train, and the last two hours of his journey enforced the sense of homecoming, for the new passengers had the familiar local accent and intonation and talked of people and of places that he knew. At the stop before Dumbridge a woman got in who said: "Why, I do believe it's young Mr. Brock, isn't it?" and told him how wonderful his mother was, doing so much yet always ready to take on more, and Edna was wonderful too, the woman added. All this was dulling to the edge of arrival. He seemed to have been arriving for hours. As he walked down the Station Road toward the High Street, home seemed to him primarily a place where he could put down his traps.

Turning into the High Street he experienced a momentary impression that there had been an air raid. Heaped on the pavements were bedsteads and fire-irons and kettles; Boy Scouts and Girl Guides were pushing hand carts laden with bundles; on the wine merchant's doorstep was a parcel of parchment-bound ledgers neatly fastened together, and from the house beyond an old woman came out who carried a bird cage and a large tolling hand bell. The Union Jack flew from the church tower. Stretched across the street, banging and bellying in the wind, was a wide calico streamer: DUMB . . . NATION . . . AGE . . . DUMBRIDGE NA-

TIONAL SALVAGE WEEK. Midway up the street was a whippet tank, so flimsy, so outmoded, that for an instant he supposed that some citizen cherishing it as a garden ornament had now relinquished it for salvage, but of course it was there to show the good people of Dumbridge what could be done with their iron bedsteads. Beyond the whippet tank was a long meandering trail, a dingy caterpillar whose meaning became clear to him as a woman's voice behind exclaimed: "Just look at the Book Mile! Where on earth have they all come from?" "What a clearance!" replied her companion.

At first he thought he would turn into a side street and so avoid this *auto-da-fé* of disgraced books laid out ready for the junk collectors. But he was too angry to spare himself and walked on, countering his distress by reflecting on the kind of books Dumbridge could muster up: *The Scarlet Pimpernel, Hints to Fly Fishers, Anecdotes of European Courts,* and volumes of poetry called *Tally-Ho* or *By Quiet Waters.* "If I see a copy of *Jessica's First Prayer,* I'll pinch it for Ives," he told himself.

So inevitably he began to look, to loiter. Montaigne's *Essays*—good Lord, who would have thought Dumbridge could produce them! *Paradise Lost*—that was not so surprising. *Letters of Queen Victoria*—oh, poor Ives! *The Collected Poems of Edward Thomas*—now who, he wondered, owning that and reading it too, for it had the unmistakable warmed look of a well-read copy, could have cast it out into a Book Mile? He picked it up. The moment it was in his hand, as though some electricity leaped from the book to the man, he knew whose copy it was. He did not need the confirmation of the flyleaf: *Edwin Brock. April, 1934.* He put it back and walked on, as though walking on would annul what had happened. But the Book Mile kept up with him; in a moment he would be compelled to open his senses again, to walk slowly, to trail his glance from cover to cover, waiting for another recognition. What tomfoolery! He would go back and rescue it. It was his book.

A voice said: "Edwin Brock, I do declare!" It was Mr. Cheeseman, chemist and town councillor of Dumbridge and old family friend. "Delighted to see you, my boy! I thought it must be you from the way you were studying those old books. You were always one for books, weren't you? Well, what do you think of it? Pretty good, eh?"

"Is there really a mile of it?"

"Well, between you and me, no. But it goes as far as the Boer Memorial. And every inch of it a gift, you know."

"People bring their books, do they?" Edwin asked. "And add them on?"

"Some do," Mr. Cheeseman said. "On our opening day you should have seen them come running out of their houses. Of course, by now it's beginning to dry up and we have to help out the look of it by books that have come in as ordinary salvage. But it's all genuine salvage, genuine Dumbridge Borough salvage, whoever puts it there. As for the old garden hoses and the brass doorknobs and the aluminium, you'd never believe it. Why, people have even brought out their medals!"

My Fitzgerald's *Letters* must be here somewhere, Brock thought; the old *Bevis* I bought when I was thirteen, and dropped into the river, and dived for; and my Nonesuch Swift.

"And every scrap of it good for something," said Mr. Cheeseman with reverence. "Every scrap of it useful at long last. You can tell the army that we're doing our best for you. Well, here we are at the Memorial. And you can see it comes right up to here. I'm going your way, as it happens, so I'll walk with you. Mill Street looks a bit naked, doesn't it, with the railings gone?"

"Yes, it does a bit."

"There's your mother waiting for you," Mr. Cheeseman said.

She was standing on the doorstep, some knitting in her hands. When she saw Edwin, she waved the knitting and then added some more stitches.

"Here's my boy!"

Her first glance was for his sleeve. No stripes—and as he had foreseen her face fell. Then, just as he had also foreseen, she reassumed that air of resolute buoyancy, the expression which in old days he and Edna had called Mother's Mrs. Greatheart, and began to tell him how well he looked, how much broader he had grown, and that she had actually got a duck for dinner, though of course it was only a small one.

"I explained to Mr. Hawes that you were coming back on leave," she said, "and he swore to do his utmost. People are so wonderfully kind! Oh, and that reminds me, Mr. Cheeseman. I can't manage Thursday, because I am at Report Centre in the morning, and then I shall be packing Prisoners' Parcels instead of poor Mrs. West—it's so sad for her that she gets these incessant colds just now—and after that I have the canteen, of course, and then the Working Party, and then the canteen again. Besides, I must keep a morsel of time for my Edwin now he's here."

She laid her hand on his disgraceful sleeve and continued to discuss dates with Mr. Cheeseman. Edna appeared. She looked extraordinarily tired, shabby, and sterile. "So you managed to get off for the duck and Edwin," said her mother.

Indoors, there was a delicious smell of roast duck and a smell of daffodils. The table was spread with a damask so white that it seemed to sparkle, and by his place was his old mug and two bottles of beer. Edna went to wash her hands.

"My darling!" Mrs. Brock said to her son. "My ducky! How I've been longing for this!" And for that moment she was quite genuine, and looked old and careworn and at the same time girlishly excited and vulnerable.

"Edna looks rotten," he said. "What's wrong with her?"

Instantly his mother began to bridle. "I daresay she's tired. We're all a little tired, you know. And then, poor Edna, it's rather depressing for her not being allowed to join up in the A.T.S. But Mr. Ransom won't release her. And as I tell her, even if she has to stay in a civilian job, she's freeing someone else, so really it's just the same thing."

"Better money, anyway."

All through the meal it was like that. A devil spoke, not he, snubbing every advance, deriding every brag. And the poor old woman, gallant and obtuse, came back every time for more punishment. Even the duck he could only praise by saying that one didn't get that sort of food in canteens, and a mention of fire-watching provoked a belittling inquiry as to how many bombs had fallen on Dumbridge—none, as he well knew, having fallen. Yet he had not meant it, and even now did not mean it. Walking beside old Cheeseman, he had settled with himself that it was no use scolding over spilt milk, that there was nothing for it but philosophy. One was always being philosophic in the army so why not be philosophic at home too, where at least there was peace and quiet to be won by keeping one's temper? But suddenly there was nothing left but to know the worst, and pushing back his chair he ran from the room.

When he came back Edna was carrying out a trayful

of dishes. His mother was sitting by the window. Her knitting was on her lap, but for once she was not knitting. She was looking at a pot of newly opened daffodils and blinking, as though their pure colour hurt her eyes.

"What's happened to my books?" he cried. "What have you been doing with my books?"

She turned to him and it intensified his fury to see that her expression was one of relief. "Your books, darling? I brought them down here, to keep dry. All the good ones—your prizes and the encyclopædia."

"Oh! " he said. "Then why did I see so many of them in that damned Book Mile of yours?"

"Oh, those were only the old things. Edna and I went through them most carefully, I'm sure. And one must do something," she added, losing her temper because she was afraid, "we poor civilians in a poor old town that doesn't even get a bomb on it. Surely you wouldn't grudge a few old books for national salvage! Think what it means to the country!"

"Why didn't you burn them," he said, "and get some fun out of it, like they do in Germany?"

"Burn them? *Burn a book?* Why, for months now we've been lighting the fires with gorse and shavings. There's no paper burned in this house, I can tell you. Every scrap of it goes into salvage. Burn a book? Why, your father's even given up his shaving calendar!"

Edwin began to laugh. He laughed on and on, like a maniac, for each idiot peal deferred the moment when he would have to decide between keeping his grudge or going out to retrieve what he could from the Book Mile.

His mother went to the door. "Edna!" she called. "Edna, take your mack. It's coming on to rain again, a regular downpour. Such a pity, on Edwin's first afternoon too!" And, returning, she knelt down stiffly before the grate, saying that on such a wretched afternoon they really must have a fire.

Step This Way

PERHAPS they stood just a trifle too long on the doorstep, but it was to avoid any appearance of urgency. The woman who had opened the door now put out a red clean hand and patted them in. In her parlour they sat down and looked at the fireplace.

"Why, I know you quite well," she said. "By sight, that is to say. You shop at the Home and Colonial, don't you?"

"Yes, we're registered there. We were at Pullock's first, then we changed."

"I've never tried Pullock's, though I know a lady who gets her tea there. Swears by them too. You'll have a cup, won't you? The kettle's just on the boil."

The girl looked at her mother and frowned. Ignoring her the mother began to acquiesce, saying it would be too much trouble, that one shouldn't take other people's rations, that it was hard to make do and worse if one lived alone.

"Don't you worry about that, I can always manage. And there's nothing like a nice cup of tea."

Saying that she could hear the kettle, she left them. They heard her in the next room, rattling crockery, opening and shutting a door that squeaked. They sat in silence. The daughter pulled a packet of cigarettes out of her bag. The mother said in a low voice: "I wouldn't if I were you." The daughter stared at her coldly and lit a cigarette. She had the grand manner of the young, she wore a hat with a little veil, a tailored suit with a coloured handkerchief displayed in the breast pocket. Her bare legs were smoothly distempered. A small gold cross hung at her neck. Beneath her make-up one could discern her natural complexion, a pure vibrating pink and white that belied all the pains she had taken to look sophisticated. The same impulsive complexion stirred, at once more violently and more sluggishly, in the large cheeks of the mother, a heavy cow-faced woman wearing a thick overcoat.

There was the noise of water pouring from a kettle, and the woman of the house came in with a tray, remarking: "This will do us all good."

She whisked a white cloth over the red one and set out the tea things. Everything was brilliantly clean, rather old-fashioned, and good of its kind.

"Ah! I see you're noticing my teapot."

They looked at the teapot.

"Quaint, isn't it? But people can say what they like, there's nothing like these old black teapots for a good brew. Gipsies, now. They'll never make tea in any other kind of pot."

"Don't see many gipsies about nowadays," said the mother in a dull unwilling voice as though the statement had been dragged out of her.

"I dare say you'd be surprised," said the woman of the house, "how particular they are. Specially in their confinements. I've often attended gipsy ladies, and it's always the same. Washed all over from head to foot, not a speck on them. And kettles boiling, as many as you could wish for. And clean rags, spotless."

"Well, you certainly do surprise me. I wouldn't have thought it, somehow. What sort of time do they have?"

"Very easy, considering. They start young, you see, and that's more natural. And how they do love their babies! Fair dote on them. Don't you like your tea, dear?"

"Very nice, thank you," said the daughter.

"But then what mother doesn't dote on her baby?"

After a pause the mother said, "Yes, indeed." But she had flushed, and looked uneasy and rather nettled.

"I'd say it to anyone, whatever the circumstances. Think of what you're missing, I'd say, the little teeth and the pretty ways and all, not to mention what it might mean to you when you're old and needing some-one to look out for you. Think it over, my girl, and don't be jumped into what may be the regret of a life-time. That's what I'd say. A wedding-ring isn't every-thing. Besides, who knows? He might change his mind. There's lots of homes that a baby has brought together. You'd be surprised."

"There's more than one mind to change," said the girl.

The woman of the house examined her hands that

were scrubbed and red and short-nailed and continued: "And nowadays, it's not like what it used to be. In the old days, I grant it freely, things were hard for a girl. People were so cruel and narrow-minded, you really couldn't blame a young lady for taking steps. But now everything's different. There's clinics, and welfare, and nurseries, every baby's welcomed. Specially in war time. Why, in war time you might almost call it a duty."

During these speeches the mother had been shifting in her chair and sighingly lifting her bosom out of her corsets and letting it slump again. Now she said: "Perhaps Mrs. Spellwell didn't fully explain."

"Make no mistake! Mrs. Spellwell explained everything. Mrs. Spellwell can always be relied on. But I don't like to hurry things." She glanced towards the girl, an anxious assaying glance. "I'd really rather not than rather, you understand. And your girl—have a fag, my dear?—she'd make a lovely little mother."

"No, thank you," said the daughter.

"It's her dad." The mother began to talk in her natural voice. "If he as much as suspected it, I don't know what he wouldn't do. He was out of work for twelve years, and that makes a man so savage. Twelve years on the dole, five kids and she the eldest, nothing but scrape and scurry, you can't call it a life! He'd say to me, 'Never mind, we're in the gutter but we're respectable.' Now, when our luck's turned and things are getting a bit comfortable, if he so much as suspected what's wrong . . . She's terrified of her dad, aren't you, Greta? Only last week he said to me, 'Mum,' he said, 'what's wrong with my girl?' God forgive me, I said it was her monthly. But he looked at me so suspicious even then. Always watching her, he is. The more so on account of Greta being so delicate."

"Delicate?"

"Why, she had to wear glasses till a couple of months ago. And her ear-ache! Whenever she catches a cold she gets the ear-ache."

"Try snuff. You can get it at Barley's," said the woman of the house abstractedly. She had lit a cigarette and through the smoke-rings she looked at the girl steadily and quietly. With her fixed goggle-eyes and her lips that rounded after each puff she resembled a fish rising.

"I think I've brought everything," said the mother. She raised a wax-cloth bag to her knees. The woman of the house was recalled to affability.

"I do hope Mrs. Spellwell explained? It must look so peculiar, I really feel I ought to apologize. But actually, really with soap-rationing what it is, I'm forced to ask it."

"Very natural, I'm sure," said the mother warmly. "I often say, of all these rationings the one that hits a woman hardest is soap. Whoever fixed the soap ration, he didn't have to do a family wash, I'll be bound!"

"And the soap's so poor too, isn't it? I don't know when I last saw a decent lather."

"A lady I know advised me . . ."

"Unless I'm to do a family wash," said the girl, rising to her feet, "you and my mother had better tear yourselves apart."

"Greta! What a way to speak!"

"I'm ready when you are," said the woman, and rose also. "That is, if you *are* ready, my girl. But it strikes me you are in two minds about it, even now. I don't want you to say I didn't give you every opportunity to change your mind, right up to the last. Several young ladies have come to me and I've reasoned with them and they've gone away like they came. And afterwards they've told me they were never-endingly grateful to me for acting as I did. So if you feel like changing your mind, even now, don't mind me."

"*She* won't change her mind." But it was the daughter who spoke.

"Greta! After all I've done for you!"

In her flurry the mother knocked over a teacup. It fell to the floor and broke. "There! You've made me go and break a cup! One of a set!"

After a momentary gesture to save the cup the woman shrugged her shoulders and turned towards the girl.

"You needn't worry," the girl said. "I won't split on you. And *my* mind's made up too. The damned woman's my mother, and I can't help that. But she won't be a grandmother, as far as I am concerned."

"You'll feel better once it's over," said the woman soothingly. "Just step into the bathroom, my dear. Step this way."

Standing so proudly on her long legs, the veiling on her hat brushing her nose with its odour of being shop-new, the girl scythed the room with a slanting glance. What was it to her, these teacups and these two old women, and all this chat of shopping and rations and washing days? And they thought themselves so clever, so managing, cunning as two spiders in a cobweb—and were nothing but two old women, soiled and shapeless. They had no power over her, whatever they did. For they were old and she was young, and they were cluttered up with fears and caution and she was reckless, scornful, indifferent as lightning.

"This way, dear," the woman repeated, a little impatiently. The strain was beginning to tell on her, and she was alarmed by the girl's looks. All that silly paint made a quite natural pallor seem ghastly. Indeed, the girl had grown very pale. Meanwhile the mother's face became redder and redder as she sat staring at her empty lap where the bag had been. It was as though by some reversal of maternity blood were draining from the child into the mother.

Daphnis and Chloe

DINGY with fatigue but still kindly, the old waiter glanced from time to time at the weather-beaten boy in mufti, the girl with a blue ribbon in her heaped-up hair, architectural as a peruke. When they came in he had snuffed the odour of moth-balls, thinking: It's his first night on leave. Now as they sat on over their emptied coffee-cups he thought: A bit of a tiff. Soon blow over.

"But I want to dance with you. All this time I've been looking forward to dancing with you."

"Dance? What about those dances in the village hall? You won't grow mouldy for lack of dancing, my boy."

"It's you I want to dance with."

"Even if we went," she said, "I couldn't dance. My knees would be knocking against each other at every step. And I won't go to the pictures either. One's as dangerous as the other. If you're so bent on dancing, why not dance at home?"

"Round and round the old aspidistra," he said, "while your Dad winds the gram and your Mum does a *pas seul* of her own, looking for where she left her spectacles. And then if a bomb drops on us we won't be killed because we're not at a Palais de Danse."

"Well . . . Why not drop in at Vanda's? She'd love to see us."

"Sure she would. Vanda'd love to see a deaf-mute with smallpox, she keeps such dazzling company. No! When I get leave I want to see life, not Vanda."

"See life? See death, more likely."

"But it's no more dangerous to go to a dance-hall than to stay at home. Why can't you see that? God knows I've explained it often enough. It's simply a question of density."

"I may be dense. But I do know what I'm talking about, and if you'd been through as many raids as I have you'd know too. But that's the trouble. You sit on your blasted heath cuddled round your searchlight and know no more about what it's like in London than a Siamese kitten that's never left Siam."

With a hand that shook with temper she tilted the coffee-pot above her cup. The coffee-pot was empty.

"I don't mean that sort of density," he said carefully. "I mean density of population. The number of people in a given place. Obviously, in a dance-hall there are more people to the square yard than there would be in somebody's quiet home farther up the street."

"It looks like it. A girl I met—she's in A.R.P. and knows what she's talking about—she told me that at Putney they dug out three hundred. I don't know if they were to a square yard or not. But they were for the graveyard all right, what was left of them."

"But because there are more people in a place it doesn't mean that they are more likely to be killed. It just means that if they are killed there are more of them. Think of it like plates," he continued. "Suppose you had fifty plates . . ."

"Why not suppose I had fifty bananas while we're about it?"

". . . and that you put twenty-five of them in a heap in the sink and distributed the other twenty-five in ones all over the floor . . ."

Her laughter was as pretty as lambs playing. Hearing it the old waiter looked round with a smile and thought: That's all right again!

". . . and then the little boy next door threw a cricket ball in at the window. If it pitched in the sink, twenty-five plates would be broken, if it hit the floor, only one or two plates or perhaps none at all."

Her laughter had ceased. She stared at a mark on the tablecloth.

"Well, it's the same with bombs. It just depends where a bomb falls. Or when it falls. If it falls on a dance-hall or a cinema it may kill three hundred. If it falls on a detached villa called Chatsworth it may kill three. If it falls on a church on Sunday it may kill fifty. If it falls on the same church on a Monday it won't kill anyone."

"Oh, won't it? You should have seen what they took out of the crypt of Saint Jude's. That was a Monday."

"I mean a church without a crypt!" he exclaimed. "But you won't even try to understand."

"I understand all right. I heard what you said. If a bomb falls on a dance-hall it kills more people. That's why we're not going to a dance-hall."

"But that's not what I said."

"It is! Only word of sense you've said this evening, it's not likely I shouldn't notice it."

"I did *not* say it!"

"You did! You said that if a bomb falls on a dance-hall more people are killed."

"But only because more people are there. Look here . . ."

"Well, I don't intend to be one of them. And I don't intend you to be one of them either. I don't want to see you killed. I can't stop you being in the army and I can't stop the war. But I can stop you from marching into death-traps, and I mean to. I don't know why you should be so anxious to get us both dead either."

"But . . ."

"Personally, I still want us to keep alive, and have a proper home and a family and some fun after all this misery."

"O God!"

"I don't understand your tony ideas about suicide. I never . . ." She broke off, swallowed violently, and made another attempt with the coffee-pot.

"Here, waiter! Another coffee for two, please."

"Yes, sir. Immediately, sir."

"No hurry at all," he said.

Across the little table they stared at each other with murder in their eyes.

To Come So Far

THE car drove slowly along the sea-front.

"There it is! Coburg House. Gorblimey!"

He was halting the car when she added with decision: "Drive on a little."

He drove on and when she said "Stop," he stopped.

"Well! Of all the mausoleums! What shall we do?"

"What would you like to do?"

"Go to Naples, of course. Or Hollywood. Or Hell. Somewhere with a trifle more life in it. But seriously, Arnold, can we really stick a week here? Or shall we ring up from a telephone booth and tell Mr. Bellowes or Burrowes or whatever his name is that we've been prevented from coming?"

He lowered the driver's window and the smell of the sea came into the car.

She said: "We'd have to pay for the rooms, I suppose. How much petrol have we got?"

He switched on the engine. "About three gallons in the tank. And another three in coupons."

"If only we hadn't come so far," she said.

He turned off the engine and looked at the sea. It was calm and heavily white and resembled a bad oil painting. Part of the beach had been cleared, elsewhere the pale sand was cross-hatched with iron posts and barbed wire where the mines were still lying. Farther along the esplanade two men were planting delphinium seedlings in a flower-bed newly dug from the neglected grass which had once been a lawn.

"Bleak, isn't it?" she said. "Oh, to be in an English seaside resort now that April's here! Oh well, I suppose there's nothing for it. We haven't enough petrol to chance going anywhere else, we can't afford to drop money on the rooms. Drive to Coburg House, dear, and let the revels begin."

But he continued to look at the sea.

Her expression changed, it became private and unobserved and at once she seemed several years older. In a different voice she said dubiously: "Or what do you think, Arnold?"

"I think it's charming," he replied. He switched on the engine, turned the car, and drove to Coburg House.

Since holidays must be enjoyed and since Arnold must be diverted ("It is what I call Black Dog, Mrs. Taverner. The Greeks had a name for it. Just now I have dozens of cases, they are very tiresome for everyone concerned and not in the least dangerous. . . ."), Cecily at once began to be pleased with their lodgings. She bounced on the mattress and commended it, she examined the pictures, she praised the polish on the mahogany. What a magnificent wine-cooler! And just look at Gladstone! All the furniture was large, but so were the rooms, large and lofty, and the walls were hung with a lustreless blond paper, the colour of the pale sea under the sallow sky.

Arnold looked out of the window and said: "I wonder if the sea here is ever blue?"

"Not very often, sir."

This was Mr. Bellowes, bringing in the tea-tray. Like his lodgings, he was tall, pale, old-fashioned, and remarkably clean.

"You see, sir, strictly speaking, this is not the sea. It is the mouth of a tidal estuary and the tide brings down a quantity of mud which clouds the water."

"But it smells like the sea," interposed Cecily. "I expect it is just as good."

"Oh yes, madam. There is nothing wrong with the ozone."

Tea was good. Dinner was better. Cecily praised it and Mr. Bellowes looked courteously gratified. He did all the catering and cooking himself, he explained, the woman only came in to clean. He talks as calmly as that, Cecily thought, of having a woman coming in to clean. Consequential old monster! She said: "Where did you learn to cook?"

"In two continents, madam. In Europe and in Asia. The Asiatics are very good cooks. They have so much patience, you see. If you have squandered years to grave a gem . . ."

It must be some quotation, she thought, glancing at Arnold to see if it were the kind of quotation he approved of. He was not listening, apparently. She went on: "And do they really sit by the fire and fan it?"

"Oh yes, madam. A very good method, I assure you. The fan acts like a conductor's baton, it brings out the sensibility of the fire."

"Yes, I suppose it would."

He gathered up the tablecloth and went out. The door had closed behind him when Arnold called him back.

"What are the cinemas like in this place? What's on tonight?"

"Well, sir, there's not much choice. There's Mr. Coward's picture—but I expect you've seen that in London. There's a French film at the Regal, a revival, beautifully acted, of course. If you care for natural history there is a nice little documentary about swallows."

"Isn't there something livelier, something with stars, something raucous?"

Mr. Bellowes said that there was an American film at the Astoria which he had heard was very good, it was about a homicidal maniac.

They went to the Astoria. As Cecily was thinking about Arnold all the time and about his malady which Dr. Woodcock called Black Dog she came away with an impression of something taking place in a cemetery and a profusion of frightful furniture; but to her relief this did not handicap her in agreeing with what Arnold had to say. He was in high spirits. It must be the sea air.

The sea air or perhaps the exhilarating way Mr. Bellowes grilled flounders kept Arnold in high spirits all the next morning. They walked on the esplanade and found an obliging dog to throw stones for. They seemed to be the only visitors at Bosebridge, for the people they encountered were obviously natives from the way they walked briskly along without looking at the sea. But a little before lunch-time there was a sudden appearance of young women—the clerks, Mr. Bellowes explained, of a Government sub-department which had been evacuated to Bosebridge in 1941 and which still occupied the three large hotels.

"What a nuisance for Bosebridge! It can't help your holiday trade."

"No, it keeps us very quiet. But there is another thing, madam, which is much against us. We were never bombed. Holiday-makers prefer a little destruction, it gives them something to look at, something congenial. A resort, like Bosebridge, which can offer only pleasure is at a disadvantage nowadays."

"Bosebridge doesn't offer resplendently much in the way of pleasure," Arnold said.

"No, sir. That is what I mean. Sea air and leisure and facilities for games and pretty scenery is not enough, is it?"

If he were married to Arnold, Cecily thought, he would not be so imperturbable, so Asiatic and serene. But those who only hear the Black Dog's bark don't fear its bite. Meanwhile Mr. Bellowes having gone away, she found herself being asked to provoke, if possible, rather less of the family butler's conversation: that is, if she could bear to live without it.

"Family butler?" she said. "Yes, I suppose that's what he used to be. And the family bequeathed him its sideboards and Gladstone and all."

"Gentleman's gentleman to some Rajah's pimp, more likely."

"Oh."

The Rajah had a pimp, the pimp had a gentleman, the pimp's gentleman had another gentleman—at that rate one would be a lifetime getting down to a butler. She was so tired that the effort of distinguishing the two gentlemen seemed almost physical. Gripping a gentleman in either hand she looked out and saw the sea and wished she could paddle; and instantly the thought of paddling brought tears to her eyes. "That would account for the curry," she said.

Arnold put down the newspaper, looked at her steadily, said "Yes," and put up the newspaper again.

O God, O God, she thought, I would so much rather have my face smashed in. She was worn out with getting on her husband's nerves, being alternately too strong or too weak—like tea. If he were a returned soldier all this would be natural. Magazines were full of stories about manly nerves unable to face the return to civilian life or articles on How to Reacclimatize Your Man, and newspapers were full of accounts of murdered wives. But throughout the war Arnold had been an indispensable civilian, jamming enemy broadcasts, and throughout the war they had got on together perfectly, complaining of the discomforts of living and giving each other expensive presents because tomorrow we die. Now in 1946, Arnold was mysteriously as indispensable as ever and they hadn't died.

Trampling on his newspaper Arnold was suddenly kneeling beside her and his jawbone was pressed to her ear and causing her agony.

"There you sit, looking so miserable and so old, and it's all my filthy temper!"

But she had seen the change of direction, his mouth swerve from her mouth and take refuge in her hair.

"It's nothing to what I shall look like when you've done playing at steam-rollers on my ear.

"Oh, sorry!"

"Don't mention it. Now say that I look happy and young, and we'll go out and paddle." She turned up her face to his scrutiny and smiled with reckless disregard for truth or beauty.

"You're crying."

"And no wonder. You've got a horrible nature and you've hurt my ear."

The first time since we came here, she thought, that he has been at ease with me. I cried, and he was at ease. If that were the answer, he could be kept happy all day.

That evening she did not talk to Mr. Bellowes. It was Arnold who provoked a conversation which began with *Sole Véron* and ended almost an hour later with astrology. Throughout the conversation Mr. Bellowes stood, shifting from foot to foot, and Cecily at intervals told herself that the real Arnold was not like this, that the real Arnold would never let a tired old serving-man stand while he sat at ease. But the unreal Arnold had not a hair of the Black Dog about him, and that night they lay together in love.

As the week sailed on she told herself that it must be the sea air, that it was too good to last, that it must be Mr. Bellowes's cooking, finally, still under a compulsion to account for it, that it must be Mr. Bellowes's conversation; for it was astonishing what a lot Arnold and Mr. Bellowes found to say to one another, and when not talking to Mr. Bellowes, Arnold seemed quite contented to listen to what the waves were saying.

In the relief of overhearing so many conversations in which she need not take part she ceased to attend to what was being said and had instead many dawdling dialogues with herself, projections of schemes for redecorating their flat and going to the ballet more seriously. One of the things insisted on by those who wrote on How to Reacclimatize Your Man and How Not to be Murdered was that wives must have interests of their own and so become more interesting. Cooking was not enough. Yet cooking was a great deal, and perhaps what was wrong with her cooking was the intensity with which she approached it. If instead of mauling old carrots through a sieve she sat fanning the gas-cooker . . . fans were also used by conjurers, they fanned a hat and elicited a rabbit. If only rabbits were not so hard to come by! A pause in the conversation made her think that some question had been asked which they were waiting for her to answer.

"I'm so sorry. I'm afraid I wasn't listening," she said, her sense of guilt so much watered-down that it was almost levity. She discovered her mistake in Arnold's face. They had not been speaking to her, they had not paused for her to speak, they had, in fact, forgotten that she was there at all.

"Mr. Taverner was saying that he prefers water-ices, madam. I wondered if you agree with him," said Mr. Bellowes.

"I like any ices I can get."

Rather aggressively she began to take part in this spell-binding conversation, which was ended soon afterwards by Mr. Bellowes going downstairs. Now the Dog will bark, she said to herself. But Arnold was sleepy and serene like any other respectable husband after a day of sea air and a good dinner.

It was not till their last morning that he told her, and even then perhaps he might have overlooked the necessity of telling her if she had not offered to pack his sponge along with her own.

"No, thank you. I'll keep it. In fact, Cecily, I had better tell you now that I don't mean to come back."

"But will they let you have another week?" she asked, not deceiving even herself.

"Not come back at all. Ever. I am going to settle here."

"Settle? The permanent parlour-boarder?"

"Not at all. I am going into partnership with Bellowes. I shall move into two rooms at the top of the house, I shall invest some capital in the business, we shall be Bellowes and Taverner, Lodging-House Proprietors, and later on we shall get a licence and start a restaurant, serving dinners only. Bellowes will cook and I shall wait. You know I wait beautifully. I am a quiet mover and I breathe through the nose."

"You certainly are a quiet mover. Just how long have you been planning all this?"

"Perhaps three days."

"I see. Oh well, I needn't pack for you, that's one comfort. I suppose you will want your things sent down, your books and so forth? And am I to go back by car or by train?"

"Cecily, please don't take it so calmly. Naturally you are furious, why can't you show it?"

"I'll show it," she replied, and rang the bell. Too late to stop her, Arnold sat down again. The bell, however, was answered by the woman who only came in to clean.

"Tell Mr. Bellowes I want to speak to him. Arnold, may I have my nightgown? You're sitting on it."

"Cecily! Before you begin to row with Bellowes—very well, before you begin to thank Bellowes for taking me off your hands, you must let me explain. You see, I like this place. I like it frightfully. It is snuffy and dowdy and pompous, and the sea is never blue, and I feel desperately at home here, I feel attached to it like a limpet. And I would like to be a lodging-house keeper. You know yourself that I am domesticated, though you have never known how frantically I have envied you when I went off every day to that blasted concern leaving you with beds to make and floors to polish and meals to cook and flowers to arrange. If I'd told you you would have murdered me—but it's true. Now at last I have the chance to lead the sort of quiet pettifogging life I want to lead, a life where I shall be doing something of my own size instead of thwarting something that dwarfs me—like Corbusier and the trees. But you aren't listening."

"I was waiting for the magic name of Bellowes. You dote on Bosebridge, you yearn to be a waiter. Doesn't Mr. Bellowes come in at all?"

"He comes in a great deal. I like Bellowes very much. I think I respect him even more."

"His venerable grey hairs, his old-world philosophy! I suppose you will sit at his feet and be his disciple and all that, and he will solve all the problems of the universe for you and cool your brow into the bargain."

"At any rate, he will admit them. He will reduce them from bogeys to realities. And you know, Cecily, that at all times, in all places, this kind of thing happens to people. You become a Trappist, or you go and live in a monastery half-way up a Chinese mountain, or you build yourself a hut beside a pond, or . . ."

Mr. Bellowes knocked at the door. Entering (he was

carrying a tea-tray), his face quite unconcealedly took on a look of concern.

"Oh, dear! I'm afraid this has been a great shock to Mrs. Taverner, sir. I don't wonder, I'm sure. These partings are peculiarly lacerating because there is not the same opiate of inevitability as when a death takes place. If you had died, sir, if you will allow me to say so, Mrs. Taverner would not be feeling it so badly. I think you should try to persuade her to drink a cup of tea."

"Another of your answers," she said. "You have an answer for everything, haven't you?"

"Not an answer, madam. There are no answers. But tea is a very good expedient, and this is freshly made."

She found that she could not look at Mr. Bellowes's face. It was at once too compassionate and too impartial. Instead, she looked at his trousers, which were old and hypocritically creased as though they were new.

"I would like my bill, Mr. Bellowes. Separately, please." She had an impression that he was gravely shaking his head. "You have made us very comfortable. And now you will go on making my husband very comfortable—even more comfortable, I expect. If any of my friends want their husbands taken off their hands and made comfortable, I shall certainly recommend Coburg House."

"Cecily!" Arnold cried out imploringly.

Mr. Bellowes said: "I shall do my best for Mr. Taverner, madam."

"I expect he's told you already that he can't eat rhubarb. Or crab. And that he doesn't like herrings, or goose, or anything made with soya, or . . ."

"No, madam."

"And I think that's all. Except to wish you joy and prosperity, and plenty of customers when you open your restaurant. When that Ministry has cleared out I expect you will have any amount of holiday people coming to gorge. You will scarcely have time to fan your fire, and Arnold will be run off his feet waiting on them. You won't know Bosebridge, it will be so fashionable, so lively, so full of people coming to enjoy your table d'hôte."

She stopped, because Arnold had caught her and was shaking her.

"Your bitch-cunning!" he said. "Trust a woman to foul what she can't understand. 'So fashionable, so lively, so full of people!' Have you any more Parthian arrows?"

"I doubt very much," said Mr. Bellowes, "if Bosebridge will ever recover what popularity it had. As I said before, it has nothing to offer but pleasure, and few people want pleasure nowadays. Being pleased is almost a lost art."

Rather wistfully he put the tea-things together and turned to the door. Then, seeing her ravaged face, he waited till she had gathered up her belongings, and silently took her away.

Waiting for Harvest

THE Borough Council of Stukely had exerted itself to comply with the British Government's request for a Stay-at-Home Bank Holiday. Among the onion beds and bean rows of the Borough Gardens (Stukely dug for victory) were swing boats and coconut shies; there was even a merry-go-round. A thin man in a light suit was playing a flageolet before a booth labelled *Marmaduke's Puppetries*, and the Mayoress, devotedly flushed, was encouraging holiday-makers to throw a ring round Hitler, three tries for sixpence, and so win a Savings Certificate Stamp.

And it was a little after midday.

Walking uncertainly Leila Cohen wandered into the Gardens, seeking diversion and an unfrequented bench in the shade. Three months earlier the Ministry of Labour had directed her into industry. Though the new factory on the outskirts of Stukely possessed every possible amenity (as the Welfare Superintendent often pointed out), daylight was not among them. And though the hostel also possessed every amenity, solitude was not laid on with hot and cold water, shower-baths, central heating, and an incessant wireless. To be alone, and in the light of day, made her feel dizzy, unsure of her feet and exposed to queer auditory illusions: just now the strong impression that some invisible clergyman was pouring loud disconnected confidences into her left ear, though with her right ear she could distinguish quite reasonably the Stukely Temperance Band, the steam-organ of the merry-go-round, and the puppetry flageolet playing "Come Lasses and Lads" with no very perceptible results.

There were no empty benches in the shade. The only empty bench was full in the sun and just in front of Marmaduke's uncompelling puppetries. She passed and repassed it several times, embarrassed by a feeling of sympathy for the thin man, a wraith from the piping times of peace and a submerged Bohemia where it was possible to wear such light suits and such little pointed beards. But at last she sat down, keeping her gaze fixed on the gravel.

A couple of minutes later the bench staggered as a heavy woman sat down beside her. The air became charged with the smell of naphthalene. Presently there was a rustle of sandwich-paper, and a smell of cheese sandwiches was added to the smell of naphthalene. Apparently this was good enough for the puppet-master. He whisked into his booth, the calico-pink curtain rolled up, and a cultured voice announced:

"Tan-tan-tara! Ladies and Gentlemen, we present Rudolfo, the Bouncing Bugler."

Still staring at the gravel Leila heard that familiar rattle of wooden joints (but now so horribly like dry bones) and some tenor toots. A fat voice beside her, additionally fattened by unswallowed sandwich, remarked: "Comical, really, isn't it?" But now it was too late to move away.

She transferred her gaze to the puppets. To the bouncing bugler, plated in tinfoil, had been added a corseted Gretchen with plaits. As the bugler bounced and tooted Gretchen skittered modestly away.

"The old, old story," commented the voice.

Three soldiers paused before the puppet-show. Three soldiers: three pairs of army boots. One of them was eating toffee, she saw the crumpled wrapper fall beside a boot.

"Wuff! Wuff! Wuff!" exclaimed the puppet-master.

One of the soldiers said morosely: "O my bloody Christ!" and the three moved on. A spotted mastiff now ramped across the little stage and Gretchen's strings were transferred to the hand that manipulated the bugler.

Beside her, extraordinarily resonant (as resonant as that invisible clergyman) sounded the *Tck!* of a tongue striking against a hard palate, and then there was a gusty sigh. More words breathed forth.

"Ah, poor young chap! We shan't see *him* again."

The dog pranced and reared. Gretchen's strings slackened and she fell in a dead faint. Another *Tck!* tolled out. Compelled, Leila turned her glance (eyes on strings, she thought) and looked at the woman, who was massive, swarthy, hairy, and wore a purple velvet ulster trimmed with rabbit ermine.

"Him on the right," she amplified. "I can read it on him as plain as a laundry-mark, poor boy! You see, I'm Psychic." And as though preparing the obsequies she smoothed out the sandwich paper on her purple knee.

"Never wrong," she continued. "And just the same in the last war, though then I was a mere Gurl. It's a Gift."

"Rather a dreadful one, I should think."

Instantly umbraged the seeress replied: "Well, I don't know about that. There's plenty as claims it, but only the few has it, I can assure you. And if anyone suffers by it, it's *me*. Definitely. *They* don't know, poor young things! They don't know it till it gets them, and very often not then. *I know*. And have to keep it penned up inside me under a bright exterior."

Suddenly and foolishly weakened Leila said: "I can partly understand that. I fill shells."

"Splendid!" Stirring out fresh wafts of naphthalene the purple mass moved nearer. "Splendid! The money's wonderful too, they say. I'd do it myself if it weren't for the kidneys. But they forbid it. Still, one has to pay for being Psychic. It drains the constitution, let alone the six other little ones coming along before, naturally weakening to mother *and* child, and always perceptible in the teeth. There! The dog's dead! Wonderfully lifelike, isn't it?"

The spotted mastiff lay inert. Gretchen revived from her faint and danced a *pas de deux* with her bugler.

"Death! But what's death? Just an ever-open Doorway, my dear. Just an illusion. Just a little step across the Great Divide. And the next minute—well, if the dog hasn't come to life again, just like I said! Quite a coincidence, isn't it? Though mark my words, there's more in coincidences than is dreamed of in philosophy."

True enough, the dog had revived, and danced on his hind legs. "And the name of the dog was Bingo!" sang the puppet-master. Amiably co-operative, the seeress sang too, and clapped loudly as the curtain fell.

"Yes, why shouldn't we be happy? They're happy, you know. I say it constantly, if clergymen knew what I know, or even believed what they preached, funerals would be more like weddings. Yes, it's been my comfort and support all my life through, the comfort I've been able to give to others. Through being so Psychic, you understand. The Messages I've passed on, in the little homely bits about terriers and old coats and what not. One dear boy said—speaking through me, of course—*Do you remember how I always forgot my umbrella? Well, we don't need to remember umbrellas here.* Oh, what a comfort it was to his mother, because as it so happened he always did forget his umbrella. Now you couldn't guess a thing like that, could you?"

The puppet-master had paused for refreshment. Leila heard him open a bottle of beer.

"How . . . do you use a crystal?"

"I never make use of any contraptions. I don't need to. I just close my eyes and Relax. Similarly, I wouldn't do it Professionally. A professional doesn't inspire the same confidence. Naturally, one can't live on air, can one? And a little acknowledgment's only one's due, like any other Gift. Just enough, I always say, to keep up my strength so that I can go on being a comfort and a Vehicle. But no more. And never professionally."

The puppet-master could be quite plainly heard keeping up his strength.

"Noisy swallower, isn't he?" commented the seeress. "Ah well, some is and some isn't. But Souls, one and all. And I dare say it takes it out of him, managing all those things and tooting accordingly. Yes, dear, as I was saying, you really might not credit the number I've been a comfort to, both here and Beyond. For they've all got something they're yearning to impart, specially the poor young things that pass over violent but have to wait for a Vehicle. Queueing-up, as you might say. The messages I've passed on, it might surprise you, so clear, and at the same time so homely. And I ought to know, having been doing it since 1918, when the Gift first came over me, just like a beautiful harmony."

"I suppose you are very busy now?"

"Well, I am. And again, in a manner of speaking, I am not. It's war time, dear, you see. And in war time the bereaved mostly keep going with canteens and savings and concerts for the troops. Not to mention those working so bravely in explosives, like you, dear. You needn't have told me that. I could read it at a glance, the moment I set eyes on you sitting here alone. That's why I came and sat beside you."

The merry-go-round had slowed to a standstill. The Lady Mayoress had paused and was sucking a lozenge. Everything seemed to have come to a stop. Leila set her teeth. The seeress resumed, and now her voice was louder and more confident.

"But after this war . . . They'll be coming to me in hundreds, just like Last Time. They'll need me then. For it's when everything is over, and life settles down, and things begin to look much the same as before except for the Empty Chair and the poor dog still waiting at the gate, so faithful and so patient, it's *then* that that bereavement Bites them. It's then they'll remember the baby ways, and cuddling at twilight, and the nasty little words they'd give anything to have unsaid. It's then they'll read the old letters and look at that little first tooth every mother keeps. And that's where I come in, that's when they'll turn to me. *Flock,* they will!"

She squirmed herself nearer. "Yes, dear, that's what it is to have a Gift. Had it ever since I was a mere Gurl. The moment I set eyes on you, sitting there so mournful in your black, *I knew.*"

"My black dress? Yes, it is shabby, isn't it? Before I was called up I played in an orchestra, we all had to wear black. And now I'm wearing it out to save coupons." She heard herself sprinkling the words lightly, like insect-powder.

In a new voice, shrill and trembling, her companion replied: "Very sensible, I'm sure. But I'd have known it, you needn't have troubled to explain. Wonderful with music, wonderful with money, everyone knows that. One doesn't need to be Psychic to know where *you* belong."

After a minute or two she rose, shook herself, and walked away. Leila Cohen watched her go. The haughty carriage soon slumped into defeat and weariness. The purple garment, too, was old and desperately shabby. She was an old shabby scabby purple tiger, trailing hungry away, having stalked a dinner in vain.

"Oh, damn the old brute!"

In a fury of compassion Leila sprang up and followed her.

The Museum of Cheats

DYING in 1692, Sycomore Hoby, Gent., a Fellow of the Royal Society, bequeathed his library and his Museum of Cheats to his native town of Tipton Bacchus, in Devonshire. He also left an endowment to cover their upkeep and the salary of a librarian who was to lodge in the Hoby house in Grace Street along with the library and the contents of the Museum.

The will was tightly drawn and contained some curious provisos: the librarian, for instance, must be a man of over thirty but not a married man; he must be a clerk but not a clerk in orders. The Museum must be open on Sundays, holidays, and all days of public prayer or general fasting from sunrise to sunset. Admission was to be free except on Mondays, when it was to cost threepence. On Wednesdays and Thursdays the Museum was to be closed, so that the librarian might have leisure to dust the exhibits and divert his mind. The name *Museum of Cheats* was to be plainly lettered upon a board which was to hang above the entrance.

The will also provided for annual payments to be made to the Master of the Grammar School and the Town Clerk, who were charged with seeing that the terms of the Hoby Bequest were carried out. The remainder of the property, apart from a few legacies to friends, was divided under trust between the uses of the parish church and the parish alms-house, with a further proviso that if the Museum of Cheats ceased to be administered according to the terms of the will this money should go to the Royal Society.

It was a local tradition that Sycomore Hoby had originally intended his museum to be called something exceedingly grand in Greek; and had only changed his mind at the last moment, when his cook, hearing him use the grand Greek word, whatever it was, had crossed herself and exclaimed: *Numny-dumny!* It is possible that this legend is true (truer, at any rate, than a variant version which holds that the museum itself was to have been called "The Numny-Dumny"); for though the will contained no word of purposes other than self-commemoratory and philanthropic, the objects bequeathed were all of a kind likely to counter such impulses as that which provoked the cook's reaction to the grand Greek word. Where other members of the Royal Society collected herbs or abounded in things petrified, Sycomore Hoby had collected objects of superstition. Living in a part of England where faith and credulity were both pretty highly developed, he had amassed a very fine assortment of bullock's hearts stuck with nails, witch-knots, hands of glory, elf-bolts, toad-skins, charms, philtres, talismans, magic pin-cushions, books of spells, waxen images, wands, broomsticks, and blessed buns. These made up the heart of his collection; but in the course of his travels he had added relics, weapon-salves, indulgences, philosophers' stones, scapulars, a couple of stuffed mermaids, one incorporating a monkey and the other a calf, an alchemist's laboratory complete with gilded nuggets, and several magnificent bits of glass from crown jewels. His library expressed the same sceptical turn of mind, consisting either of exposures of cheating or of works of piety and hermetical treatises liberally annotated by himself. Five folio volumes bound in calfskin contained his detailed catalogue of the collection.

During the eighteenth century the Museum of Cheats enjoyed a considerable amount of local esteem. The house, being newly built, gave no trouble, the rents came smoothly in, and there was no lack of unmarried secular clerks of over thirty to keep up the supply of creditable librarians. From time to time the clerks were so totally secular that they kept mistresses under the same roof as the mermaids; but as there happened to be no exact directions about such a state of things in Sycomore Hoby's will, nothing could be done or was done about it.

In 1728 the Museum of Cheats missed a distinguished visitor. Sylvester Tull, the current librarian, wrote an account of it to a celebrated foreign writer, then in London, and begged the honour of his inspection. But the letter received no reply, possibly because he had addressed it to Monsieur Arouet instead of to Monsieur de Voltaire. In 1737 there was a regrettable loss of a blessed bun, which was forcibly removed by a Mrs. Sabina Cranch, who said that she needed it for a difficult delivery she was in charge of. Ezekiel Almond, the librarian at the time, found it vain to show her the relevant entry in the catalogue which exploded the whole theory of blessed buns, since Mrs. Cranch could not read. When he assured her that there was not a tittle of evidence in favour of even a superstitious application of blessed buns in breech presentations, Mrs. Cranch said that she had been using blessed buns before he was born; and that his own coming into the world might have left him looking less like one-ninth of a tailor had such a bun been exhibited on that occasion. Finally he was compelled (he was indeed a poor figure of a man) to let her carry it off, though he got her promise to return it. But she did not; and in the end, being threatened with the law, said it was impossible, the cat had eaten it.

In 1763 the Museum of Cheats was involved in an affair of honour. The neighbourhood had long been disquieted by two eminent archæologists, Mr. Melhuish of Badworthy, who wrote in *The Gentleman's Magazine* under the soubriquet of Cato, and Mr. Blaze of Lewcombe, whose contributions to the same journal were signed Arbiter. Between them Cato and Arbiter had burrowed into every tumulus within miles, demolished hoary pigsties in search of Roman remains, traced Hadrian, Cassivelanus, and Boadicea all through the county as though they were foxes, and unearthed centres of Druidical worship as fast as the followers of Mr. Wesley put up meeting-houses. Naturally these enthusiasts suspected each other's circumspection; but they were civil enough to go on referring to each other as merely misled, ill-informed, credulous, opinionated, childish, and senile, till the day that Cato found a Druidical staff of office—and found it stopping a gap in one of Arbiter's hedges. The account of this discovery, made on the property of Mr. Blaze of Lewcombe, gentleman, was read by Arbiter with fury. He, a gentleman? A gentleman, like any other Squire Booby? Concealing his fury (he was as furious as that), he waited until Cato's attention had moved to a newer discovery, stole away the staff, and privily conveyed it to the Museum of Cheats. Then he published a description of it in *The Gentleman's Magazine*, pointing out the many remarkable resemblances between it and the staff recently discovered by Cato; and mentioned where it could be inspected by cognoscenti.

Cato immediately challenged Arbiter. They fought with swords on a very wet morning, and both gentlemen returned much scratched and cut about, and by no means as satisfied as they declared themselves to be.

Bartholomew Cary, the librarian, was in hot water for this—and not much bettered by his defence, which was that though he had noticed the Druidical staff he had taken it for an old broomstick left by the cleaning-woman. There was talk of dismissing him. But, as had happened before when causes for scandal had poked up their heads, the Town Clerk and the Master of the Grammar School could not agree. There is something about being yoked together, under even the lightest of yokes, which makes agreement very difficult. The Town Clerk was of the opinion that Tipton Bacchus had been made a laughing-stock, and that Mr. Cary was responsible and should go. The Master of the Grammar School said that if the Town Constable had arrived in time to arrest the duellists Tipton Bacchus would have been no more and no less a laughing-stock than it had been for the last ten years; and suggested the Town Clerk should replace that doddering old Coffin. Meanwhile the cleaning-woman was dismissed for being so careless, and (since she was a good poor woman with a long family) her eldest daughter took her place.

This girl, Anne Moxom, was one of those women of character who made the eighteenth century so agreeable. In a higher walk of life she would have been a Madame du Pompadour or a Mrs. Thrale. As it was she had to content herself with learning Latin and studying Anglo-Saxon. She corresponded with Mrs. Chapone and Mr. W. Cole, she wrote an account of the antiquities of Tipton Bacchus and a dictionary of the Devonshire dialect. She also kept the Museum of Cheats so sweet and clean that people went there for pleasure. All this was well enough; but when Mr. Cary died Anne Moxom must needs apply to become librarian in his stead, and had the effrontery to claim that Sycomore Hoby would not have made any objection on the ground of her sex, basing her claim on some of his annotations to the works of the Fathers of the Church. At this both Town and Gown were in agreement, and Anne Moxom was sent packing. She went to London, and presently came on the town, and that, you might suppose, would be the end of her; but she bobbed up again as the celebrated Mrs. Despenser, who kept none but educated whores.

On the centenary of the Museum of Cheats the living quarters of the librarian were renovated and improved and a feast was given to the Grammar School children and the inmates of the alms-house. This became a yearly custom, and could well be afforded, as the value of the Hoby property had gone up considerably.

In 1820 Town and Gown again found themselves of one mind. Tipton Bacchus had been severely visited by a fever epidemic, at the same time there had been a murrain among cattle and the Corn Exchange had been struck by lightning. The Reverend Mr. Mugwell, B.A., curate of the parish (the rector was absent at the time), suggested that these occurrences might have been provoked by the sins of the parishioners, but no one paid much attention to his view till it was seconded by Triptolemus Hard, the Converted Pigman, who said the same thing with such eloquence and with such lively assurances of more and worse to come that Tipton Bacchus totally forsook Mr. Mugwell and prayed in the fields with Triptolemus for days on end. Even when they had tired of Prayer they did not desist from Works.

One of the Works undertaken was a universal demand that God should no longer be annoyed by the Sunday opening of the Museum of Cheats. As this necessitated repainting the sign-board (days of prayer and general fasting were of course included with Sundays) advantage was taken of this opportunity to revise it a little further and bring it into better accordance with contemporary good manners. The words *Museum of Cheats* were still painted on the board, but they were painted very small, and painted above them, very large, were the words *Hobyeian Repository*. At the same time the fee for admission was increased to sixpence and the free days reduced to one day a week.

Possibly as a result of this, possibly because of the march of time and its inevitable concomitant of an increase of human wisdom, the Museum of Cheats came to be looked on as more and more old-fashioned and ridiculous. No one visited it except children and a few holiday-makers who went in to giggle at the mermaids and to come away with a general sense that in the days of yore everyone was very gullible and Sycomore Hoby especially so. As for his catalogue and his annotated books, the volumes slumbered on their shelves, and the post of librarian would have become one of the most sought-after sinecures in England if there had not been so many others to choose among and if Tipton Bacchus had not been such a dull little town in one of the wettest districts of the West. As things were, it afforded a congenial and padded seclusion to, successively, Alfred Tregurtha, 1822–1839 (*Tregurtha on the Prophecies, Tregurtha on the Seven Vials,* etc.); Decimus Pine, 1839–1850 (*Anecdotes of Missionary Travel, Thoughts on Female Youth,* and *Life of Wilkinson*); Horace Godweed, 1850–1880 (*The Coleopterist in Fact and Fancy*).

The repose of Mr. Pine was rudely interrupted by a visit paid to the Hobyeian Repository in 1843 by a Mr. Hickey Colville. Mr. Colville, a young lay disciple of Dr. Newman's—none the less earnest for his laiety—had come down with a reading party to the neighbourhood of Tipton Bacchus during the long vacation. It was—as usual—a wet summer, and Mr. Colville was an exhaustive scholar. Thus he not only read the whole sign-board outside the building, but a great deal of the detailed catalogue within it. The upshot was a letter to a local journal in which he protested very strongly and mystically against the exhibition of Sycomore Hoby's collection of relics.

"For wherein"—the letter concluded—"does the essential nature of a relic consist? By no means surely not only in the bare origin of its being, but also and with infinitely more significance in the sense in which it is received—which is, in the case of a relic, the distinguishing piety of the worshippers. In this sense every relic is a reliquary, an outward and visible sign of an inward and spiritual grace: i. e., the faculty of worship; and consequently the reverencing of relics, even of relics which may be patently insusceptible to authentication, is not merely licit and commendable, but the duty of every Catholic."

For many nights after this letter had appeared Mr. Pine imagined the course he would take if he should have the pleasure of finding Mr. Hickey Colville living up to his sentiments and reverencing exhibits nos. 57–65 of the Hobyeian Repository. He even had them dusted and moved forward to abet the process. But Mr. Colville did not oblige him. He had gone home to his mother, who lived at Penge; and Mr. Pine's frustration gave him a stomach-ache which lasted for months and seriously interfered with his *Thoughts on Female Youth.*

Mr. Godweed, on the other hand, was not in the slightest degree diverted from his insects when Mgr. O'Downey remarked in a public lecture that the display of the Hoby pseudo-relics left him as a Catholic unmoved, only Anglicans fussed over such things; but that he could wish that the glass rubies, etc., from European crown jewels might be withdrawn, such things created a bad atmosphere and encouraged Liberalism—he was not referring, he hastened to add, to English Liberalism, but to the Liberalism which stalks under that name through the continent—which every loyal heart, whatever the religious persuasion, must naturally abhor.

Mr. Godweed was succeeded by Robert Emerald,

who wrote neither on religion nor on insect life. Reputedly a man of much learning, Mr. Emerald wrote nothing but poems in such forms as the triolet and villanelle, and published but very little of what he wrote. He was not a man of his time. In an age of Imperialist expansion he knew so little of the Empire that he admitted quite freely that he had no idea as to the whereabouts of Uganda.

One of the results of Imperialist expansion, of course, was the enormous development of private collections. There was scarcely a gentry house within hearsay of Tipton Bacchus which had not got its full quota of rhinoceros horns, poisoned arrows, quaint gourds, bottled scorpions, boomerangs, cowries, Javanese marionettes, etc.; and the opening up of China added to these a number of objects of value and virtue from the Imperial Palace. Apart from objects of value, which soon settled down in new homes, these innumerable demonstrations of the vastness and variety of an Empire on which the sun never sets began to present quite a Congested Districts problem to the neighbourhood. It was one thing to send your younger sons to the colonies; but no sooner had you cleared out the sons than a trickle of curiosities flows back, and before long there is not a small spareroom which has not a trophy of poisoned arrows and a couple of Buddhas in it, not to mention the insect life which accompanies so many of these curiosities, especially if the colonial labours have included big-game hunting. Crushed beneath elephants' feet, encumbered with beaded aprons, eaten alive by silverfish, the families of the district began to cast eyes of covet on the wide, open spaces of the Museum of Cheats; till little by little that too was colonized: by presentations, by objects on loan, by bequests, by all the known expedients of dumping.

At first Robert Emerald kicked. But the tide of events was too strong for him, and after a few years he was as amiable as you could wish, receiving every new increment with the polite exclamation, uttered in a dry whistling voice: "Most suitable, I declare! This is something quite after old Hoby's heart."

By the second centenary of the Museum of Cheats the original Hoby collection was in a sort of native reservation in the cellars, and every other square foot of the building was taken up by the burden of Empire. As for Mr. Emerald, he had relinquished villanelles and was absorbed in composing a detailed catalogue of the recent additions: ten mss. volumes, every one of which perished in the fire which also put an end to Mr. Emerald and to the contents of the Repository apart from the Hoby stuff in the cellar, which escaped with but little damage. It would have been ruined, of course, and everything else preserved, if the hose of the town fire-engine had not been so unfortunately perforated in so many places.

The fact that the Museum of Cheats rose from its ashes in the year 1905 was brought about by the old antagonism of Town and Gown. Gown, on this occasion, was Mr. Elphinston, B.Sc., a forward-looking man who felt strongly that the time had now come to use the Hoby money for a useful purpose: viz., a new full-sized laboratory for the Grammar School. Town was Mr. Cranch (probably descended from the Mrs. Cranch who removed the blessed bun, and certainly connected on the distaff side with the Moxoms). His feelings were conservative, he wanted the Museum as before, and he worked up a good deal of sympathy. Many citizens of Tipton Bacchus convinced themselves that the happiest hours of their childhood had been spent in the Museum, and that life without mermaids was emotionally blank. Three neighbouring families offered to lend their grounds for a bazaar. But this died down again; fathers of families said that their boys would get more out of a new scientific laboratory than from a pack of old oddities which nobody believed in; and once more the three neighbouring families repeated their offer about a bazaar. Finding that it could not be done peaceably, Mr. James Cranch resolved on sterner methods. He called a town meeting and read the terms of Sycomore Hoby's will, laying a good plain stress on the clause which directed that if the Museum of Cheats ceased to be administered as was laid down, the moneys divided between the use of the parish and the use of the almshouse should go to the Royal Society.

The Royal Society is a scientific body and, as its name implies, under royal patronage; but not the most ardent devotee of science nor the loyalest church-going Erastian in Tipton Bacchus was willing to contemplate all that good income diverted to something that went on in London. Even if they had been, the alms-house committee and the churchwardens would have shouted them down. It was carried *nem. con.* that the Museum of Cheats should be rebuilt; and the remainder of the evening was quietly spent in a speculative discussion of architectural styles.

With that mistrust of the outer world which had made Tipton Bacchus what it was, it was agreed to do without any architects, and to commission Mr. Hawke the builder to keep the shell of the house and make the new museum as like the old one as he could manage. With Mr. Cranch keeping an eye on him Mr. Hawke managed a very passable reconstruction, the new notice-board announced Museum of Cheats with no word of repositories, the free days were as Hoby had ordered, and the price of admission went back to threepence. The Sunday opening had to be waived. Mr. Cranch knew where to leave off. The Lord's Day Observance Society was one of these boundaries.

In 1912 a charge of sixpence was made for admission on Saturdays. Now that so many people from God knows where were flying about in motor-cars with money to throw away, it would have been flouting providence to disregard them. An article on the Museum was published in a London paper. Photographs of the mermaids were sold on picture post cards. An enterprising firm of local potters designed a Hoby Jug, and had just launched it when the outbreak of war obliged them to turn their minds to sterner things, like pudding-basins.

Specimens of the Hoby Jug are now extremely rare, and when Justinian Bogey (librarian, 1922–28) found one he made it the centerpiece of his private collection. Tipton Bacchus had chosen Justinian Bogey with the most exalted motives: was he not an ex-service-man, and one-legged at that? At the interview too, he had seemed a very quiet, indeed rather sorrowful, young fellow, who had renounced the world and grown a beard. What no one could have foreseen was Mr. Bogey's friends—either young artists in corduroy trousers or middle-aged ladies in ropes of pearls, all devotedly attached to each other and to Justinian Bogey. For six happy years Tipton Bacchus watched them as one might watch a circus; for either they were letting off fireworks or reciting poetry or constructing grottoes or leading about bears or buying second-hand gas-brackets or sprinkling salt on their strawberries or something equally unforeseen and harmless. Seldom have exalted motives produced such a lastingly pleasurable result. When the American lady married Mr. Bogey and took him away everyone was sorry and life much the poorer.

Inside the Museum of Cheats too, Justinian Bogey and his circle had a most vivifying effect. Though at first no one quite knew what to make of the new decorations (designed and applied by Mr. Bogey's friends), the lime-green walls, pink wainscots, and allegorical ceilings were eventually approved, and even imitated by some of the younger people of the town who were setting up house for the first time and wanted something that did not remind them of home and Flanders. The mermaids, readjusted and new-stuffed, were set out with appropriate backgrounds of shells and anchors; the relics were regrouped in a handsome maplewood cabinet (the gift of an anonymous friend); the wands and broomsticks were de-wormed; the alchemical laboratory was put into working order and once a term the senior science class at the Grammar School came and worked it.

In the course of time some of Sycomore's specimens had decayed. Mr. Bogey's widespread friends filled the gaps. In addition, there was a small display of Exhibits on Loan. These were chosen with the greatest eclecticism, and sometimes it was quite a puzzle to know why such familiar objects, household words you might say, should be there. This was the case when Mr. Alistair Lothbury, O.B.E., a newly-arrived land-owner, found among these temporary exhibits a copy of Mr. Baldwin's work, *On England.* "I suppose," he said, turning it over to see if it were a first edition, "I suppose this got here by accident." Justinian Bogey replied that surely no one who knew Mr. Baldwin could doubt for a moment how it had got there.

When the American lady had taken away Mr. Bogey, Mr. Lothbury—who for a little while had contemplated taking away the American lady—continued to hang round the Museum of Cheats, wistfully welcoming any revisiting friends of Mr. Bogey's and giving every assistance in his power to the new librarian. For by now the Museum of Cheats was, in this gentleman's words, quite definitely worth one's attention—and worth, apparently, quite a lot of money too. Some figures about insurance, lightly spraying from Justinian Bogey, had astonished him.

There is no reflection more galling to those whose ancestral background has not afforded a great deal of cupboard room than that almost anything, if you can keep it long enough, becomes vendible. The vendibility of Sycomore Hoby's junk was a thought at once delicious and tormenting (like love to Catullus) to Mr. Lothbury. Those books, for instance, that nobody read or could read, those philosophers and Fathers of the Church—they were, it appeared, all first editions. The very pins in the magic pin-cushion were handmade. Above all, the alchemical outfit was unique and inestimable; yet that fool Bogey, while he had sense enough to insure it properly, had allowed the boys from the Grammar School to play with it (this, however, in the name of culture, Mr. Lothbury had managed to put a stop to).

With the country entering a period of economic depression (Mr. Lothbury would have felt it irreverent to use the word slump) the vendibility of the Museum of Cheats increasingly preyed on his mind. It was obvious to him, and he tried to make it as obvious to others, that a good patriot like Sycomore Hoby would not have hesitated to sell a few of his whatnots if by doing so he could have eased the burden on the local rates. The mere fact that he was dead should not be allowed to stand in the way of doing on his behalf what he would, if alive, have done himself for his native town which had meant so much to him. And then Mr. Lothbury would quote the example of other distinguished patriots, even then patriotically engaged in disposing of family portraits in order to abate the death-duties. Not content with talking of sales, Mr. Lothbury even found buyers; in particular, a German gentleman, deeply interested in alchemy, who was ready to buy the alchemical outfit lock stock and barrel and pay a really remarkable price for it. Town might have yielded. This time it was Gown that held out. Mr. Elphinston, bald now, and wheezy, with nothing of his tartaned origin left to him except the way he sniffed, held to the letter of the Will, threatened with the Royal Society as if the threat were entirely his own invention, and added privately that Tipton Bacchus had better look out or that Lothbury would be helping himself.

But, in fact, it was the unfortunate librarian who, dazzled by all this talk of untold gold, absconded in 1936 with two relic-cases and a Rabelais.

This occurrence led to the formation of a Committee of Management, a step long advocated by Sir Alistair Lothbury (knighted in the Jubilee Honours), who was, however, ungratefully omitted from the list of the chosen. The Committee was made up of the Rector,

Colonel Pugh-Carew, T.D., J.P., Mr. Melhuish, J.P., Mrs. Vivian, Mr. Howard Hawke, of Hawke and Son, Mr. Luscombe, the respected butcher and grazier, and, *ex officio*, the Town Clerk and the Master of the Grammar School. With rather indistinct ideas of what to do they did their best. Their ideas were indistinct because their directive was so explicit. They could not believe that all that was required of them was to assure the exhibition of a number of objects chosen to insinuate the notion that man is liable to be made a fool of. Accordingly, they discussed—and abandoned—a series of ameliorative red herrings, such as a series of lectures on subjects interesting to an agricultural community (insect pests, pasteurization, etc.) to be given on winter evenings and which might counter the tendency to go to the cinema and gloat on High or Western Life; an exhibition of home handicrafts by the Women's Institute; the installation of a wireless to broadcast selected items from the Western Regional Programmes of the BBC; the production of German's *Merrie England* or a Nativity Play; folk-dancing; rabbit-craft; and the purchase of a (reputed) portrait of Sycomore Hoby, attributed to Lely. The only suggestion that could legitimately be pursued came from Mr. Luscombe, who pointed out that no building is indestructible and proposed that every year they should put by part of their revenue to form an Emergency Fund.

In September 1939 everything became much clearer. The contents of library and museum were packed, put in the cellars, and heavily sandbagged. The librarian, Mr. Charles Colet, went into the army. The building was taken over as a Recruiting Centre till it was requisitioned by the War Office about a twelvemonth later.

When Charles Colet came back to Tipton Bacchus in March 1945 (he had spent two years with the Maquis and six months in a sanatorium), his first impression was that the Museum of Cheats had suffered from a near hit. Its windows were broken and boarded up, the door was gone and its place was taken by some strands of barbed wire. Being still imperfectly reacclimatized to civilian life he cut this and walked in, and found himself in an oddly familiar world of hacked woodwork and crumbling plaster. The nature of the sentiments carved on the wainscot and the unexpected enrichment of five bath-tubs explained what had befallen.

Howard Hawke saw him walk out and came up for a word of welcome. "Did you ever see such a shambles?" he inquired. "Lord knows what my poor old dad would have thought about it."

"What about the collection?"

"All that's down in the cellars still. It ought to be all right. Mrs. Vivian had the keys, and kept a pretty sharp eye on it. Went and blew up a major single-handed when a tap was left running. Did it handsomely too, so I heard. Pity she's going. But her grandson's killed and she's giving up the place and going to London. Mr. Melhuish is off the Committee, too. It had to be him or the Colonel, they fought so in the Home Guard. And Lothbury's on."

"Who's responsible for that?"

"Well, in a manner of speaking, me. You see, he's got so much pull. It will take pull if we are to get the order taken off and get the stuff for repairing it, and not be from now till the next war doing it. Have you ever seen anything in such a state?"

"Yes," said Colet.

That evening he tossed up to decide. The coin came down tails. Tails he stayed. He had arranged with the Town Clerk to put in a few days examining the collection and the books; but instead of the keys he got a letter. His generous offer was not quite feasible. A few months longer in storage could not hurt the objects, the hour of victory one might now safely say would not be long delayed. To do anything just now might prejudice the Committee's position *re* the authorities, which Sir Alistair Lothbury had so well in hand. Everything possible was being done and would continue to be done. As for the dry rot, there seemed every reason to hope that it was not so extensive as Mr. Hawke anticipated. And Colonel Pugh-Carew, Secretary to the Hoby Advisory Committee, was his sincerely.

More was lost at Mohacz. Colet went off to Edinburgh and spent the summer reading in the Public Library. Early in September he received a curt letter from Colonel Pugh-Carew saying that the Hoby House was now re-opened and that the Committee would be glad to know when Mr. Colet proposed to return and take up his duties. The style of the letter, Colet supposed, might be accounted for by the election. The style of Hoby House called for more thought.

If on his previous return he had supposed that the building had narrowly escaped a bomb, his first impression now was that the Museum of Cheats had just been visited by some minor royalty. Streamers of patriotic bunting flapped on it, over the entrance was a composition plaque of a bas-relief bulldog uncomfortably inserted in a capital V, and from within came the loud strains of the wireless broadcasting the Waltz from *The Swan Lake*. Otherwise there was a total hush. He walked in. The total hush was corroborated by a total absence of humanity. On the walls hung enlarged photographs of babies in napkins and sometimes in necklaces, together with feeding-charts and essays on the vitamins. Presumably it was some sort of itinerant exhibition.

He walked into the second room. This contained a table-tennis table, some dart-boards, a number of chairs, and one sleeping man. Meanwhile the Waltz from *The Swan Lake* had been succeeded by a talk on How Christians Can Play Their Part. He listened long enough to discover that, as usual, the creator was badly in need of a little assistance and could not be expected to do everything single-handed. The second room, like the first, was newly done up in a manner that vouched for Sir Alistair Lothbury's pull and Howard Hawke's technical efficiency. They looked pretentiously homely, and perfectly frightful.

He went up to the library, which was on the first floor. This had not been redecorated. The shelves were sprinkled with cups and saucers and mysterious little bottles containing heeltaps of methylated spirit. Banners leant against the wall, and in one corner was an old hat-box from which paper garlands overflowed. Everything was dirty, and a dirty cretonne overall hung on the door. He went on to his own quarters, and found the door locked. He went downstairs and seated himself opposite the sleeping man. Presently the man woke up and asked if it were still raining. It developed that he was in charge of the Child Welfare Exhibition, and that it was not attracting many visitors. Later on, the man said, a few people might come in to play darts; but not many, what could you expect in a place that had no licence? In his opinion, he continued, the whole thing was nothing but a cheat, opening up a barrack of a place like this as a recreation centre without as much as a canteen in it, and the housing shortage a scandal.

Late that night, having got his keys and settled into his quarters ("I had to make out with bits and pieces," explained Mr. Hawke, "for the licence wouldn't stretch to all I had in mind"), Colet went down to the cellar. The sandbags had rotted and a landscape of dunes covered the cellar floor. Cases reared forlornly out of it, like wrecked and land-locked vessels. There was a pervading smell of damp and decay, and he began to remember Mr. Hawke's story of the tap which had been left running. He pried open a case. It was the case containing the relics—exhibits nos. 57–65. They had not suffered much. As relics they were less emotional than the newspapers in which they had been wrapped. It was odd to read on such substantial paper such insubstantial sentiments: *England Had No Quarrel with Germany. Return of the Bustle. Confidence in Business Circles. England Expects . . . A Short War.*

He put them back again and opened the second case. It held books, and a dolorous smell came out of it. In spite of Mrs. Vivian the running tap had done its work. The books came out of their discoloured wrappings swollen and blained, like the dead. From the third case such a stink arose that he had to sit down and reason with himself before he could go on. *Only a woman's hair.* Only a bullock's heart.

Walking to and fro, trying not to be sick and not to rave, trying not to recall other hearts in other cellars, Colet fixed his mind on Sycomore Hoby, Gent., Fellow of the Royal Society, and comfortably dead for two and a half centuries, who had drunk wine from these very cellars and walked admiringly among his *hortus siccus* of human credulity, human vileness, human despair. If he could see his collection now, poor old billy-goat, what would he think? In a flash of realization Colet knew what the dead man would have thought. This was no *hortus siccus* to him. To him, in his day, these cheats, these exploitations, these articles of faith, were mouldy, slimy, disgraceful—stinking then as now. He had collected them with detestation and bequeathed them with purpose.

One result of this midnight meditation was that in the subsequent transactions between the Advisory Committee and their Curator (the term Curator had been substituted because, as Mr. Luscombe remarked, Librarian wasn't a term that meant much nowadays), the behaviour of the Curator impressed the Committee as being inconsistent and hard to account for. On the one hand, Colet made a positive nuisance of himself about the books and the objects: insisting on unpacking them, and taking it on himself in a most arbitrary way to get them restored with all possible expense. On the other hand, he took the loss of the two main rooms—or rather, their new public-spirited utilization—quite quietly. Though he was overbearing about the library, insisting on it being put into repair and making the provision of refreshments even more difficult for the devoted ladies of the Women's Institute, he seemed quite ready to fall in with the new order of things in which he lost the two free days which had been his under the old order of things. And while his manner was detached to the point of insolence and though he inflexibly refused to take the slightest interest in the developments downstairs, he did not once refer to the terms of Sycomore Hoby's will.

But of course, as the Secretary said to the Chairman, Colet would think twice before endangering his hold on a job which carried a free lodging with it.

This was also Sir Alistair Lothbury's reading of the enigma. He was much obliged to Mr. Colet for his obliging frame of mind, and peculiarly grateful to be spared any rumpuses just now. He, too, was anxious to retain his hold on an excellent advertising frontage.

The result of the election had not been such a shock to Sir Alistair Lothbury as to many of his friends. What made him very thoughtful was the result in the local constituency, a safe Conservative seat, where the Tory candidate had got in with a majority of two hundred. Sir Alistair Lothbury thanked his stars that he had not been in a hurry; for though, of course, he had backed the fellow, and sat on his platforms and all that, it was in a non-political way, an expression—no more—of the deep veneration he felt towards the country's great Leader, Mr. Churchill. One might as well suppose that the composition bulldog over the entrance of the Hoby House was political. In many ways, as he remarked when discussing the result of the election, he was himself a Socialist, just as Mr. Churchill was in many ways a Socialist. More effective measures of Socialism had been put through under his guidance, etc., etc. A balanced Socialism, preserving all the best elements of the past and yet keeping its eye on an organized future, was in his opinion the policy the country needed, and its surest safeguard against any infection from Moscow. He was second to none in his admiration for the deeds of the Red Army—once it had got on its feet while we in the West were keeping the ring for it—but war wasn't the same thing as peace. In short, Sir Alistair Lothbury was preparing himself to be the Labour candidate in the next election—unless any contra-indications turned up meanwhile.

In this contingency his attention riveted itself more warmly than ever upon the Museum of Cheats. In the past his feeling for it had been almost boyishly idealistic: the idea of so much money locked up in whatnots of no intrinsic value had appealed to his imagination, fidgeting him with impracticable day-dreams. Such day-dreams unreciprocated by tangible results naturally lose their interest; they pass into a maturer outlook, a sense of deeper values. The Museum of Cheats, a mere receptacle for gilded nuggets and glass rubies, was succeeded in his mind by a Hoby House and the far more thrilling alchemization of mass appeal. In opening the renovated building Sir Alistair Lothbury explained how the Hoby House would now become what Sycomore Hoby had really intended it to be: the vitalizing heart of his native Tipton Bacchus, constantly pumping out a life-giving stream of all that was best in the latest ideas, and combining with them opportunities for relaxation which we all must need after these proud but gruelling years of dogged endurance.

The reopening ceremonies included a life-giving stream of cider-cup and went off resplendently. Rather too resplendently, perhaps, for a fortnight later, during which fortnight nothing had streamed but some rather exhausted cocoa provided by the W.V.S., the Hoby House was a palpable flop. There were even some malcontents who inquired for the mermaids.

Such inquiries were easily turned backwards and put to scorn. Almost unprompted by Sir Alistair Lothbury the Town Clerk and the Master of the Grammar School, both devout Labour men, discerned the inherent unprogressiveness of wanting mermaids. Had Labour swept the country, had Fascism been overthrown, had Major Attlee got there at last, for nothing more than a reappearance of mermaids? From wanting mermaids it was but a short step to abolishing the Trades Unions and returning to feudalism. Meanwhile the Rector, skating the troubled waters like a water-spider, was rather foolishly going round saying that if people really wanted the mermaids it might be possible to squeeze them into the Children's Corner of the parish church, and Colonel Pugh-Carew wrote the letter which brought Colet back from Edinburgh.

The Rector and Colonel Pugh-Carew were not the only members of the Advisory Committee to feel rather pensive about Sir Alistair Lothbury's manipulation of the Museum of Cheats. Mr. Hawke was extremely uneasy; the more so, since it was he who in a professional anxiety about dilapidations and dry rot had invoked Sir Alistair Lothbury's pulling powers. Mr. Luscombe, too, was troubled in mind. It might be all right, but again it might not; and one thing he felt sure of, if Mrs. Vivian should take it into her head to come back she would make it most unpleasant for all concerned. But in these perturbations the members of the Advisory Committee recollected that it was really no business of theirs. The Hoby Will had appointed the Town Clerk and the Master of the Grammar School to see that the testator's intentions were carried out; if they raised no objections no one else could. The Master of the Grammar School, a newcomer to Tipton Bacchus, short-handed and overworked, knew nothing of the Will except that it brought him twenty pounds a year and had provided a fund to give an annual feast to the Grammar-School children, which fund, growing unwieldily large for its purpose, had been diverted to the upkeep of playing fields and the provision of silver cups and other athletic equipment. The Town Clerk knew the Will better than that; and having once been a solicitor's office-boy he could not help remembering that the law is the law. But he had no doubt that they were acting in the best interests of the town, and shared the general feeling that the end of the war and the change of government had changed everything and put the past securely in its proper place. Besides, it wasn't as if they were dealing with a down-at-heels concern which might at any moment go bankrupt and be inquired into. Far otherwise. And then consider all the good that was done in the name of Sycomore Hoby: the alms-house, the church so well dowered that alone of the churches in the rurideconate it paid its way. Meanwhile Messrs. Govell, Govell, Weir, Nancy, and Kensit of Bedford Row continued their priestlike task of sending in very neat statements of credits, debits, and professional expenses twice yearly.

Early in 1946 Mr. Colet reported that all the salvageable contents of the museum and library were in order and displayed on the first floor. The Chairman thanked him cordially and sent a little notice to the local papers. He also agreed that in order to avoid any misapprehension it would be quite in order for Mr. Colet to hang a small notice-board, with the words *This Way for the Museum of Cheats* at the foot of the staircase.

Quite a number of the older inhabitants of Tipton Bacchus went upstairs to renew their acquaintance with old friends. The room was a trifle crowded but for all that Mr. Colet somehow found space for a display of Exhibits on Loan, such as had been inaugurated by Justinian Bogey.

On April 1 Mr. Colet asked permission to make use of his own wireless from time to time in the library. Some unusual guardian spirit impelled Sir Alistair Lothbury to ask why. Mr. Colet said that sometimes there were talks on regional or rural features, such as the Helston Furry Dance, Harvest Homes, Blessing of the Crops, etc., which he hoped might help the Museum of Cheats to come alive to its patrons. Still unwillingly (for the unusual guardian spirit still bothered him), Sir Alistair Lothbury said he could see no real objection, provided the wireless was kept down and did not interrupt the dissemination of the Light Programme downstairs.

Mr. Colet's wireless was kept down; but increasingly the repose of the ground floor was broken by people marching upstairs to the library and by bursts of hearty laughter coming from thence. Not unnaturally the theory was promulgated and even accepted that in some way the patrons of the Museum of Cheats had got around the licensing laws and were enjoying themselves with more than darts, table-tennis, and Brains Trusts in which Sir Alistair Lothbury took such an active part. At odd times explorers went upstairs to see what was going on so merrily. But all in vain; somehow the glasses were spirited out of sight, the fumes of alcohol dissipated, the indecent photographs shut up in the religious books. All they found was a group of their fellow-citizens soberly listening to broadcasts by professors, clerics, members of Parliament, or the BBC's own staff of experts. And yet these same sober listeners as they came downstairs later on looked as if in some unaccountable manner they had been entertained.

By the early summer the disparity between those who enjoyed the life-giving stream of all that was best in the latest ideas downstairs and those who dropped in to the Museum of Cheats had become so marked that even Sir Alistair Lothbury (whose various mind was just now deeply occupied with the plight of the British Housewife) had to notice it. He spoke about it to the

Town Clerk, who asked with asperity what did he expect, with the mermaids on view at all hours, pandering to the weaker side of working-men in their hard-won leisure. The worker, he added, is only a human: here he stopped abruptly, remembering that the *locus classicus* for this irrefutable statement might glue him to a political past which as a loyal member of the Labour Party he was most anxious to live down.

Sir Alistair Lothbury remarked that this was a point of view which he would certainly go into; and a few days later said to Colet that the Committee, while fully appreciating their Curator's devotion to the Museum of Cheats, feared that he might be overtaxing himself by keeping it open after six P.M. Mr. Colet replied that he had to be about anyhow, in case he was called on to adjudicate in a dispute at darts or supply extra chairs for the Brains Trusts, and as the contents of the Museum were insured in the present advantageous rate on the understanding that they would not be left unguarded, he could see no alternative. Sir Alistair Lothbury inquired why the devil he couldn't lock the place up. Mr. Colet answered that to do this would not be in accordance with the wishes of the founder, as made plain in his Will.

Under different circumstances Sir Alistair Lothbury would have taken pleasure in overriding this quibble. But Colet looked at him so nastily and spoke of the Will with such malevolent suavity that he could do nothing beyond emitting some wistful thanks.

On his way home he remembered some alterations needed in his garage, and told Mr. Hawke to come and give him an estimate. Mr. Hawke came. One thing led to another, and the estimate had swollen to the dimensions of needing a building licence before Sir Alistair Lothbury, gliding sideways on an allusion to the masterly way Mr. Hawke had repaired the Hoby House, commented on the popularity of the Museum of Cheats and asked Mr. Hawke what he thought was at the bottom of it. Mr. Hawke said that he put it down to education. People were more educated than they were in the old days. He quite enjoyed a bit of education himself from time to time.

He thought he had managed this wonderfully. He was, in fact, so much elated, that on his way home he stopped to tell Colet how he had put old Lothbury off the scent.

"Education, I told him. Education. That'll keep the lot of them away, I thought to myself."

"I wonder you didn't say culture," said Colet.

"Durn it! I went and forgot he."

Colet said that he dare sayed education would do.

Pépin had told him that in the early days of the Resistance, just as in the first year of the war in Spain, advantages amassed with an infinity of care had to be thrown down the drain and good lives lost because an immature rank and file that has not learned caution, on first seeing it displayed, suspects it to be cowardice. Yet caution cannot be taught theoretically, the advantages and the lives must be hazarded. Leaning out of his window, smelling the lilac and looking at the dove-coloured roofs of Tipton Bacchus, he did not smile at the disproportion between the sort of thing Pépin had in mind and in his own small affair. True, he was handling a much smaller gun; but the target was equally the same. He did not even have to make up his mind, circumstances had made it up for him.

When they had clattered upstairs and settled down to listen he watched their faces. They had certainly come on. To their native dislike of being fooled his expositions had added a more impersonal hatred of imposture and even a certain discrimination against balderdash. Their bursts of laughter were less self-consciously loud and less frequent. Some of them did not laugh at all.

Among the party on the other side of the door was Mr. Walter Cranch, who was there most unwillingly. He had twice been invited to join the Advisory Committee and twice had refused. He would sit on no Committee under the chairmanship of that blackguard, he had said, leaving it to Mr. Luscombe to word his refusal more currently. Mr. Walter Cranch was an old-fashioned and very honest man, and at this moment he was in a raging temper: with himself for yielding, with his companions for persuading him to come and eavesdrop on a stairhead. Beyond the door the calm voice proceeded with its account of that day's proceedings at the Whitsun Conference of the Labour Party. Mr.

Cranch looked round in triumph on his companions. All this fuss and nonsense about a few chaps listening to the news.

His foot was on the stair, he was about to stamp himself off when someone beyond the door giggled briefly. The Town Clerk pursed his lips. Mr. Luscombe parted his lips. Mr. Cranch stiffened, and stayed where he was. Presently the BBC reader broke off and gave the air to a record of part of a speech. The speaker was rolling up to a climax, a loud imperious statement of what he would do and what he would not do, and every sentence was armoured and bristling with personal pronouns. He had just asserted his exemplary intention not to exploit hunger as a political factor, and had clinched it by the use of one of those stark old biblical substantives which carry such lofty and yet such homely overtones of our Puritan forefathers, when the recorded voice, loud at it was, was obliterated by an outburst of unquestionably genuine laughter.

Before anyone could stop him Mr. Cranch had thrown open the door and disclosed the stairhead party.

"It's outrageous!" he exclaimed. "You ought to be ashamed of yourselves, the whole lot of you! It's outrageous, and I tell you I won't stand it. Call yourselves Labour, and sit here laughing at Mr. Bevin!"

Howard Hawke leaped up. "Come in, one and all," he said. "Your place is on this side of the door. Come in and make yourselves at home in the Museum of Cheats!"

As this is my first personally conducted mess-up, thought Colet with slightly hysterical calm, I had better learn what I can from it. So he stayed in the window-seat till the news broadcast came to an end, when he rose and turned off the wireless, and went back to the window-seat again, which he shared with the monkey mermaid. She, too, seemed to be studying the proceedings with the saddened attention of an evolving intellect, and a dispassionate observer would have seen the resemblance between the man and the monkey. But there were no dispassionate observers just then.

Meanwhile, as no one had closed the door which Mr. Cranch had thrown open, the people of Tipton Bacchus who chanced to be relaxing themselves downstairs became aware of an unaccountable shindy overhead. They heard Mr. Luscombe declaiming about wolves in sheeps' clothing misleading packs of young noodles, and Tony Belchamber retorting that he was glad to hear Mr. Luscombe give such an accurate description of what in his latest bill he had entered as Easter Lamb. They heard young Coffin stammering about freedom of speech and young Mrs. Coffin referring to someone unknown as a Perspiring Toady, and old Mrs. Seymour who kept the toyshop and was young Coffin's redoubtable mother-in-law saying she wasn't too old to learn and so far there wasn't a law against it either. They heard the Master of the Grammar School demanding at short intervals to be informed whether or no Howard Hawke wished to imply that he was a cheat, and Mr. Cranch repeatedly assuring Mr. Colet that though he disagreed with every word he said he would fight to the death to preserve his right to say it—which was the more puzzling since Mr. Colet had not been heard to say anything whatsoever. They heard the Town Clerk saying he would root every Pink out of Tipton Bacchus and that he stood four-square behind democracy and referring to Finland and serpents establishing themselves in key positions and then taking the workers' hard-earned money for it, and Howard Hawke asking him how he had enjoyed his last lot of Sir Alistair Lothbury's hard-earned peaches, and the Town Clerk inquiring why Mr. Hawke had been so keen to get Sir Alistair Lothbury on the Committee, and what he made out of it in the matter of one-inch boards, and Mrs. Seymour intervening with an injurious anecdote about a contract for the town drains.

By this time people had begun to drift in from the street to find out what was going on. So when Howard Hawke, raising his voice to a scream, invoked old Hoby's Will and said that rather than put up with any more hanky-panky he would bring a lawsuit and let all the Hoby money go to that Royal Society and Tipton Bacchus be damned, the silence that followed these words was broken by a disorderly and spontaneous cheer from below-stairs; for odd as it may seem the townsfolk of Tipton Bacchus were well aware that there had been malpractices over the Hoby Bequest, strongly resented it, and were quite prepared to see justice done, since the particular heavens which would in consequence fall would be the Advisory Committee, the alms-house, and the church, whose fates were perfectly indifferent to them.

By the morning everyone knew what had happened and everyone was agog to see what would happen next. What happened was that the Hoby House was found by the District Surveyor to be unsafe, was closed for repairs, and still remains closed. It is understood that when these repairs are carried out the contract will be in the hands of a London firm.

A Beaver Muff

AS SHE rounded the door with the tray her glance swivelled to the bed. His hand on the red quilt looked quiet enough, but he said: "Pug, do get me a nightgown, a crêpe de Chine nightgown."

Her epoch, her breeding, had made of her the kind of young woman who is prepared to deal with emergencies. She put down the tray, smoothed back her hair, and said that it would be quite all right, she would see to it. Her knees knocked together and she felt a passionate desire to be far away, eating an ice cream in some unknown secure place. But it was only delirium, influenza cases often become delirious, doctors think nothing of it.

"Heavy crêpe de Chine, hand-faggoted throughout. But I can't make up my mind whether it should be lavender-blue or eau de nil. My eyes . . ."

He sat up and looked at her. Perhaps it was not delirium. Besides delirium there are complexes, and after the repressions of war . . . But complexes can be dealt with, they are part of modern life, and analysts take them in their stride. Above all, one must deal with them quite naturally and unreproachfully.

"*I* think lavender-blue," she said. "Eau de nil is rather tartish. How do you feel about a little jelly?"

"I feel I'd like a lot. I'm hungry. I'm revived by reading about the desperate rich in *The Times*. Pug! We must take *The Times* regularly, even though it's threepence. Sit beside me and listen to this."

He put his arm round her waist and began to read aloud.

" 'Crushed white velvet evening model, suitable winter bride. 30 gns. Electric blue ditto, trimmed sequins, cleaned, 25 gns. 6 pairs suntan silk stockings, 18 gns. Heavy blue gentleman's overcoat, 44 chest, 12 gns. Engine-turned gold cigarette case, holding 5, electric razor, 3 pairs white polo breeches, bottle exotic scent in gift case, pair hemstitched linen sheets.' Lord, what a happy pair! But they've got to part with it all. Now where are those nightgowns? 'Pink satin and elastic suspender belt, quantity ostrich feathers . . .' "

"I like this one," she said. " 'Gentleman, 6 ft. 2., requires trousers, tweed, corduroy, waist 44. Also small pair of bellows.' "

"Oh, he's just an escapist, he's going to live in some ingle-nook in Cornwall. 'Gold lamé evening wrap, lavishly trimmed baby leopard.' "

"I suppose they're all ladies' maids, really," she said. "How outrageous! Here's a bitch asking nine guineas for a pair of bedroom slippers. Négligée . . . kilts . . . Do these people never wear any *reasonable* clothes?"

He looked at her smooth head, at her smooth flushed

cheek. Pug would never want any but reasonable clothes, and it was a pity. Here was all this spoil and ruin, fine feathers falling from scared birds, London going the way of Rome and Byzantium and Pekin, and all a-blowing and a-growing and for sale in the Shopper's Market Place column of *The Times*; but Pug unmoved, Pug austere, Pug only unbending to read it because he had influenza and needed a little diversion, or so she thought. But at the moment his fever had left him, he was merely a young man in a bed.

"No coupons," he said, like Satan whispering in Eve's ear.

"I should think not, at those prices!"

"Well, would you like a model steam-engine? Or some Imperial Tokay?"

Because he was convalescent, languid as a serpent, and full of malice, because he had nothing to do but lie in bed and plot stratagems, because the bedroom wallpaper was faded and the eider-down had a patch on it, because his pyjamas being new were necessarily of the kind called Utility, and because a year ago he had been moving among ruined cities and dead men and writing poetry with the greatest ease and now with all this opportunity on his hands could not write poetry at all, Inigo Williams was determined to entrap his wife into lusting for something unwarrantable. Pug was not such a fool that she did not see his intention, but she was fool enough to admit seeing it; she gave herself into his hands when she pointed out so triumphantly that the lambskin boots were three sizes too large for her, that the street suit by Molyneux was only to be inspected in its Mayfair home.

"No, of course. It would be ridiculous to go to London. Besides, I'm so much better now that I am not well enough to be left. Discerning Pug! Well, you won't get your suit after all." *And I take your Queen,* he added to himself. "But aren't there any trusting gentlewomen who will send things on approval if we send them a great deal of money first?"

"A doeskin waistcoat, a corsage of gardenias, and an M.A. hood and gown," said poor Pug, gambolling round the snare.

"Better luck tomorrow."

Tomorrow or the next day. She was so nearly caught that he was losing interest, and it was only from Don Juanism and having a bet on it that he caught her off her guard with five yards of pure Irish linen, intimidated her with a sky blue débutante's négligée trimmed with apple blossom, and finally pinned her down to a beaver muff.

On her way to post the deposit cheque Pug alternately reproached herself for being ungracious and assured herself that the damned thing could always be returned. On her way back she began to think that a beaver muff, a small melon-shaped beaver muff, might be rather nice. But Inigo appeared to have completely forgotten all about it—unless she had silenced him by her ungraciousness. At intervals she offered up small bright references to the muff, and he answered them, but no more. Like something she shouldn't have eaten and couldn't digest, the muff squatted in Pug's subconscious mind, and this humiliated her a great deal, for sensible people do not allow themselves to be victimized by trifling obsessions. When four days had gone by without bringing an acknowledgment of the cheque the trifling obsession was replaced by a life-sized suspicion of swindle, and she was thankful to see Inigo go back to work, for with Inigo out of the flat she could distract her mind by giving the bedroom a good turn-out and distempering the kitchen. Two days later the parcel came.

It came by the midday delivery, while Inigo was out. It was a remarkably shabby parcel, the brown paper was creased and the string an assortment of odds and ends knotted together, and it was not till she had opened it and plunged into quantities of tissue paper and a smell of lilac that it occurred to her that here was the beaver muff.

However, it was not the beaver muff. It was a pair of rose-coloured corduroy trousers. As she unfolded them, out fell a card on which was written in a young and curly hand: *So sorry, the muff's gone. Would you like these instead?*

Trembling with virtue and rationality Pug shook out the rose-coloured trousers and growled at them. Her disappointment about the muff and her annoyance at finding herself disappointed and the recollection of all she had gone through, worry about the cheque, remorse towards Inigo, flooded her with eloquent thoughts about the idiocy, blatancy, and social undesirability of people who could make no better response to the emancipation of fifty per cent of humanity's legs than to deck them in rose-coloured corduroy. "Strolling about like a pack of worthless flamingos," she exclaimed; and the tissue paper rustled at the vehemence of her words. But this was unjust to flamingos, whom Nature attires in pink for useful sexual purposes, at least that is one explanation. Flamingos do not flaunt their pink in idleness and unproductivity, like fox-hunters.

And such fine material too, and such workmanship, all wasted on fripperies! So she began to grieve over the rose-coloured trousers and to feel a sort of apostolic concern for them, and to measure them against herself. They seemed to be the right length. A pair of even rose-coloured trousers is inherently more constructive than a muff. The material, soft and thick and supple as chamois-leather, would last for years. They would gratify Inigo, who liked luxury. Eventually they could be dyed.

She pulled off her grey flannel slacks and pulled on the rose-coloured trousers. They went up her legs like a caress. The caress hesitated, became constrained, jibbed. The rose-coloured trousers were too tight for her, too small in the waist, too narrow in the seat.

She had refolded them in their tissue paper and parcelled them squarely and efficiently before she asked herself what she was to say to Inigo. On the heels of what she should say to Inigo (and whatever it was it must be hearsay only, on no account should Inigo and the trousers meet), she recollected that she must also say something to the vender. She undid the parcel and took a sheet of Inigo's best paper and wrote on it: *I regret that these are not what I want. Please return the cheque.* Then she did up the parcel once more and took it to the post-office. The sun was shining, and all the way to the post-office she could watch her shadow: the shadow of an active, useful member of society, thickening round the buttocks with every constructive step, every co-operative bend. And as for Inigo, she had decided to wait till he asked.

He did not ask till the next day. By then she was able to tell him pretty exactly what had happened, and to remark that she was no sylph, and dreadfully mortified.

"Serves us right," he said, "for dabbling in Goblin Market. I don't suppose there ever was a muff. Or else it would have turned into a few dead leaves next day."

His poor Pug! He had led her all this dance for nothing. But there is no outwitting of Destiny, and Pug was definitely not destined to luxury. Meanwhile he was rather pleased to think the cheque was coming back; for in the interval he had begun a pursuit of a young woman who was—though in every other way inferior to Pug and she would not last long—the kind of young woman it is pleasant and easy to spend money on.

Bow to the Rising Sun

"SOME girls," said Miss Doris Butt, assistant to Mr. Caldecott of the Borough Fuel Office, "would get married right away and start a baby. Not that I should find it so difficult, but I'm not the sort of girl that would. I shouldn't feel it right, somehow. Would you, Mrs. Stanley?"

The older woman murmured that she wouldn't, and went on searching through the file labelled "Memos from Ministry."

"Though, of course, it wouldn't apply to you, would it?" Miss Butt said.

Again the older woman murmured her agreement. At nine A.M. she had become a clerk. It was now noon, and it seemed to her that during the last three hours she had gained considerable insight into Miss Butt's private life but regrettably little into the running of the Fuel Control Office.

"No, of course not," Miss Butt said. "For one thing, you're married already, and for another you're over the age. Can't you find it?"

"It doesn't seem to be here," Mrs. Stanley said.

"Never mind. Maybe it isn't. Maybe I put it into Pending. Dear, dear, I'm afraid you'll be rather lost without me! But you won't be the only one. Poor Mr. Caldecott, he'll be quite a lost soul really. You see, he depends so much. Of course, it isn't as though I were going into the A.T.S. When Mr. Caldecott called me in and told me that, try as he would, he really couldn't get me deferred again, he said to me, 'Now, on no account, Miss Butt, are you to worry. I'll see you don't get sent into the A.T.S.' And I said to him, 'No indeed, Mr. Caldecott. I'm sure you couldn't bear to think of my legs in khaki stockings.' Of course, you see, having worked for him so long, I can say that sort of thing to him. It cheers him up, I dare say. I expect he'll miss me. I'm always so bright, you see. A smile for everything and everyone. Besides, I understand him. Still, it's got to be. My King and country want me. That's what they said in the last war, isn't it?"

"Yes," said Mrs. Stanley.

"Those last-war songs are having quite a comeback, aren't they? They're a bit hymny, but swinging them puts more life into them, doesn't it? I can't abide anything without life in it. I suppose you can remember the last war quite well? And I wasn't even born then. Somehow it seems funny, doesn't it?"

"Is this it?" Mrs. Stanley asked, handing her a mimeographed sheet.

"Yes, that's it. That's what you've got to go by now. So you'd better cast your eye over it."

Mrs. Stanley began to read. Miss Butt began to sing. Her voice had an appealing youthful roughness. Like the fubsy down on young bracken shoots, thought Mrs. Stanley trying to concentrate on Kitchen Nuts and Bath and Bristol Coke.

"Then there's anthracite," Miss Butt said. "Anthracite's tricky."

"Why?" Mrs. Stanley asked.

"Well, you see, it's mostly the better people who want it, people with furnaces, and they generally leave it to the last moment and then come in about it. I've got a list of them somewhere, but I expect I've mislaid it. You see, I know them so well. There's Miss Stebbins and the Reverend Cash and Miss Rylands—oh, she's a nuisance, that Miss Rylands! Comes in covered with shopping and says, 'Where's the Fuel Controller? I want to see him personally.' And poor Mr. Caldecott, he absolutely dreads the sight of her, and I have to invent no end of excuses. Mrs. Grandison—she's nice, she is—old Colonel Prowse, Viscount Abington, Mr. Hume-Pinney. Oh dear, what a shock it will be to them when they come in expecting to see me and find you! Lots of them bring me flowers. They know I'm so passionately devoted to flowers. But Mrs. Grandison generally brings eggs. Well, I suppose you've read all that by now. Now you might as well enter these up. It'll all help to give you an idea of the hang of things."

Miss Butt leaned back and began to polish her nails.

"Knowing how to manage them," she said presently, "that's the important thing. It just makes all the difference. The day I was called for my interview I heard

Mr. Caldecott ringing up the Labour Exchange. 'You ought to send Miss Butt into the Diplomatic Service,' he said. 'She's got the human touch.' Of course, I do think he exaggerates. I'm not so marvellous as he makes out. I just don't bite their heads off the way he does. Still, you've got to have the human touch, though personally I've always found people perfectly sweet, especially the better sort of people, you understand. They come in raging, but somehow I soothe them down and they go away all smiles. There's Mr. Hume-Pinney, for instance. Well, last month he came in and he said to me, 'Button'—lots of them call me Button, sort of short for Butt, and me being so tiny, it's natural—'Button,' he said, 'why have you sent me coke? I thought you loved me.' 'Why, yes,' I said. 'Wasn't there a message pinned to that coke—*With Love from Doris?*' And believe it or not, he went off perfectly happy, and it never even came out that Mrs. Grandison really had got his coal. Actually, you see, I'd got their applications mixed up. I suppose that's what Mr. Caldecott means by the human touch. And that's what you'll have to concentrate on, Mrs. Stanley, if you want any peace in this job. Otherwise it's squabble, squabble, squabble, the whole time. Of course, I do admit it's a bit of a strain, always being a little ray of sunshine, but—you can take that call."

A moment later Miss Butt snatched the receiver out of Mrs. Stanley's hand. "Good morning, Colonel Prowse . . . Yes, it's me. It's Miss Butt speaking . . .

What? . . . Oh dear! Your greenhouses again! You know, what you need is a coal mine all of your own, really it is. Of course, we can't promise anything absolutely, but . . . Yes! That would be best. You come in and explain it all."

Putting back the receiver Miss Butt flew to the window-sill, removed some rather exhausted daffodils to the waste-paper basket, and emptied their vase out of the window. Then she straightened her table a little and flicked some dust off the filing cabinet. Glancing at Mrs. Stanley she seemed for a moment to contemplate freshening up the older woman's appearance too. Instead she sat down and began to renovate her make-up, busy as a kitten cleaning itself, and for five minutes was perfectly silent.

Then, with newly reddened lips, she began talking once more. "Now Colonel Prowse, who'll be coming in presently, is just what I've been saying. In fact, Mr. Caldecott says straight out he's one of my conquests. Personally, I think he's rather an old dear. But you've got to take him the right way, you know, and be sympathetic about his old greenhouses and not mind his jokes, which are a bit Anglo-Indian, I admit."

Mrs. Stanley put a stencil in her typewriter and began to type. Miss Butt raised her voice. "Copying that memo now? You *are* taking hold, aren't you? Of course, I dare say when you're here it will all get more official. Everyone thinks I look such a baby, and I expect that's one reason why people like Colonel Prowse tend to make rather a pet of me and think me so marvellously efficient. Not that I'm anything out of the way, I'm sure. I'm just nice to them and of course I never forget a face, and I've got a sense of humour. That's my little secret really. How to win friends and influence people. Do you know, there was a book in America called *How to Win* . . ."

The door opened. Miss Butt sprang up, radiant and condescending.

"Good morning, Colonel Prowse."

"Good morning, Miss Butt."

Looking up from her stencil Mrs. Stanley wondered why he had been referred to as old Colonel Prowse. Erect and trim, he had an appearance of indomitable middle age, and he carried a large bunch of pink carnations with almost completely successful assurance.

Miss Butt's glance slanted over the bouquet. Still holding it he said: "It's about my greenhouses, Miss Butt. I've just made over another of them for tomatoes and I must have extra heat. I've got a Land Girl, I've got some fertilizer, and now all I need is a little heat. Eh? Do you see my point, Miss Butt? Of course you do. You see everything, clever little girl that you are. So now, what about it?"

"Well, Colonel Prowse, I'll certainly mention it to Mr. Caldecott when he comes in this afternoon. After all these preparations you do deserve a little encouragement, don't you?"

"I'll say I do." Colonel Prowse nodded. His glance

flickered over towards Mrs. Stanley, an examining, questioning, disparaging glance.

"Colonel Prowse, I've got something to break to you," Miss Butt said. "Something terrible!"

"Eh? What's that?"

"You're losing me, Colonel Prowse. You're going to lose your Button. I've been called up."

"Good Lord!"

"Yes, they can't do without me any longer. Things must be pretty desperate, mustn't they, if they can't do without poor little me?"

"Rotten," Colonel Prowse said. He was now studying Mrs. Stanley more attentively.

"Never mind, Colonel Prowse," Miss Butt said. "You're going to have Mrs. Stanley instead. And I've just been telling her she must be specially kind to you."

Still holding his flowers Colonel Prowse moved across the room. "How do you do, Mrs. Stanley? I hope Miss Butt hasn't been prejudicing you against me. I try not to be more of a nuisance than I can help."

"Yes, I've been putting her wise about you. The gipsy's warning, you know."

Now he was standing by the typewriter. "Well, Mrs. Stanley," he said, "I hope you won't find it too bad here. You know, I think it's pretty marvellous the way people like you take on these awful jobs. I can see you know all about typing though. That's a lovely bit of work you've got in there. It's a pity you shouldn't have a nicer office. It ought to be done."

"Well, Colonel Prowse, and what about beginning with my poor empty flower vase?" Miss Butt said.

"Eh? Oh yes! Flowers," Colonel Prowse said. "Yes, I generally try to bring a few flowers along to sort of brighten things up. These are nothing much, I'm afraid. But I've got some tulips coming on, and then there'll be roses. I'm rather proud of my roses."

He laid down his bouquet by the typewriter and said: "Well, I mustn't keep you ladies from your lunch. So it's good-bye, is it, Miss Butt? Best of luck, and thanks for all you've done for me. You'll remember about my little business, won't you, and put it through with Caldecott? Or perhaps I should ask Mrs. Stanley to see about it?"

After the door had closed and the brisk footsteps died away Miss Butt said: "Don't you think he's rather sweet? So touching, the way he brings his flowers along and then gets all shy about them and dumps them down anywhere. Well, thank God it's lunchtime. We'll go to the Old World, shall we? Want to wash your hands? You go first."

In the washroom Mrs. Stanley found herself crying, weeping unavailing tears for the desperate idiot valour of the young.

"Boors Carousing"

IT WAS still raining, it was half-past two in the afternoon, Mrs. Gainsborough had gone home and would not be back till she came at half-past six to see about his dinner. He had his house to himself and the long afternoon before him.

No one would come interrupting in, the rain would see to that. Though country neighbours too often look on a snow-storm or an easterly gale as prevenient to a rousing walk and a call round about tea-time, this was summer rain: it would keep them at home, disapproving—though irrationally, since the rainfall of an English summer is higher than the rainfall of an English winter. But they were not governed by reason.

He walked into the hall and took his telephone receiver off its stand. It began to utter the soft duteous growl it would keep up till Mrs. Gainsborough came and replaced it. He stood listening to the only noise in the silence of his house: a heavenly and nourishing silence. No little footsteps on the stairs, no little smears of jam on the stair-rail. Magdalen and her brats had torn themselves away that morning. True, in the loving moment of riddance he had sketched an invitation for Christmas; but Christmas was a long way off and by then, he hoped, his brother-in-law would be out of his job in Army Education and enforcing his natural dislike of intellectuals. All through his lovely empty house rang the noise of the rain, singing in the gutters, lisping against the window-panes, plashing on the flagged walk; and in his mind's ear he heard the most melodious rainfall of all, *l'eau qui tombe dans l'eau,* the rain falling into the swollen river that washed the foot of his garden and tugged at his Chinese willows. To look through the windows of a Georgian house at a Chinese view . . . He sighed with contentment at his lot and went back to his library.

With a whole afternoon before him in which to write it would be slavish, he thought, and sinning his mercies, to begin to write immediately. He would read for a little first. The act of reading, the effacement of mind in a kindred mind, *l'eau qui tombe dans l'eau,* puts one in the best frame for the act of writing. He would read for a little, then he would settle down to write; and seriously, working on his philosophical novel where he aimed to apply the narrow brush of Jane Austen to a Tiepoloesque design: for the charms of philosophy are usually obliterated by a style of revolting romanticism, all tufts and vapours. With Magdalen in the house he had found it almost impossible to get on with the novel, he had written short stories, a prey to human nature which is poison and dram-drinking to the serious artist.

Half an hour later he put down his book, saying "Damn!" A knock on the front door had resounded through the house. Sitting motionless he listened, and presently there was another knock.

"Blast these people who can't see the bell!" he muttered. Life in the country had taught him that there are two kinds of visitors: those who ring the bell and those who knock. Those who ring the bell are at least semi-educated and can be relied upon, after three or four rings, to use their wits and go away. Those who knock are the poor and humble, accustomed to being kept waiting, accustomed to being ignored. With the pertinacity of the downtrodden they are capable of knocking for an hour on end.

A third knock sounded, no louder than the first. After an interval, no longer or shorter than the previous intervals, there was a fourth knock. Exclaiming: "And in five months' time it will be the carol-singers!" he rose and marched off to open his door.

"Oh, Mr. Kinloch! I see it's you, Mr. Kinloch. I am so sorry . . ."

"Do come in."

"No, no, I wouldn't interrupt you for the world. I just came to ask you—such a silly question, really. Do you think it will go on raining?"

"Undoubtedly, I should say. Do come in."

"I said to myself, I'll just run up and ask Mr. Kinloch. I felt sure you'd have a barometer. I'm Miss Metcalf, you know."

She was wearing a sou'wester, and the rain poured off

it, and from under the brim and behind the raindrops she peered at him like an elderly mermaid, he thought, who had taken to country life. Her name was Metcalf, and she was a maniac. So far, so good.

"Miss Metcalf," she repeated. "I live down by the river."

Dort oben wunderbar. He repeated his invitation to come in.

"I don't know if you've noticed how the river is rising. All this rain, of course. I'm so worried about the rabbits. There are eight young ones."

He said that probably their doe would look after them.

"But she can't. She's in the same boat. At least it's a coop really, a sort of coop."

"Dear, dear!" he said. "But I wish you'd come in. You are getting so needlessly wet."

She stared at him desperately.

"It only needs lifting. If it could be lifted on to the table, for I always keep a table in the garden, it's so nice in summer and one can put things on it, everything would be all right. But it *is* rather heavy, and the rabbits get so nervous and rush about like a shipwreck . . ."

"I'll come at once," he said, dimly and gloomily realizing an appeal to his manly strength.

At his gate there was a moment of awkwardness, for he turned to the left and set off briskly towards the village. She followed him, tugging at his sleeve.

"It's the other way, Mr. Kinloch. I'm Miss Metcalf, you know. I dare say you thought I was Miss Hancock. *She* lives by the church."

They turned about and splashed down a lane and across a sopping meadow where an indeterminate track led into a grove of willows and alders which was also, apparently, a rubbish-tip for the village, since some old iron bedsteads and disused oil-heaters glowered rustily among the tree-trunks. Beyond this, suddenly and surprisingly whitewashed and neat, was Miss Metcalf's dwelling, like a bandbox abandoned on the river's brim by someone who had committed suicide. And the river, just as Miss Metcalf had said, had risen enough to be washing over its banks and round a large rabbit-hutch. He clasped the hutch—it was revoltingly cold and slimy—and lifted it on to a table.

"It seems a pity," he said, for somehow he had to overcome her pelt of thanks and apologies for having troubled him, "to keep such a handsome mahogany table out of doors."

"Oh yes, Mr. Kinloch, I often think so myself. But what am I to do? There is no room for it indoors and it belonged to my father. He was the rector, you know."

So that was who she was! He had often heard her story and no doubt he had heard her name as often; but the two had become disconnected in his memory. Miss Metcalf's father had been the Reverend Thomas Metcalf, sometime Rector of this parish and now resident under a very ornate and informative tombstone;

which did not, however, mention that he had drunk himself and his fortune out of existence, which was why poor old Miss Metcalf lived where and how she did and was a trifle eccentric, you know.

But it seemed to him a charming place to live, if one did not object to being flooded from time to time and kept oneself uncompromised by rabbits. Her view was better than his own: for one thing, it included his house, and at exactly the right distance to be seen at its best. Fortunate Miss Metcalf, who could gaze down the river all day at his south elevation, while screened from the world by her thicket of willows, alders, and old bedsteads! No one would ever come knocking at *her* door. A time might come, a time might come too easily, if the housing shortage continued and he could no longer fend off impertinent inquiries as to how many bedrooms he had and whether he did not feel quite lonely all by himself in such a large house, when he might be very comfortable here. He did not suppose she would live for ever—and surely she and her rabbits would be much better off farther—so to speak—inland.

Meanwhile Miss Metcalf had become somewhat sprightly and was asking him in for what she called "just a wee drappie." It was now too late to refuse, so he followed her under a trellised porch that was like Niagara, and past what he believed to be a mangle to her parlour. Anyhow, he was pleased to, for he wanted to see the inside of her place.

There was this much to be said for it, it was totally

unrestored, and with a very small expenditure and the right kind of fixings one could make the room very agreeable indeed. He noted the alcoves on either side of the hearth, their shelves now sagging beneath cloth-bound divinity and The Badminton Library, but worthy of his Montesquieu, and the latticed windows, so very jessamy, and the delicate original fireplace hidden behind that appallingly burly anthracite stove. One could make of it just such a room as De Quincey enjoyed those winter evenings in—omitting Margaret and the ruby-coloured laudanum. Of course one would have to put in drains and electricity and that sort of thing. Meanwhile he sat compressed between a sable sideboard and a portentous table with an oil lamp in its centre, and opposite him sat Miss Metcalf, backed by a harmonium, and offered him a cigarette. No wonder she kept tables in the garden. He had never seen so much furniture, and all so frightful, in his life. The room was icily and cleanly cold, and smelt of honest poverty. How on earth she cleaned it, how on earth she scrubbed the encumbered oil-cloth . . .

Miss Metcalf remarked that she would have a little one too, to keep him company.

Yet the room did not look damp, it was just because she kept no fires.

"How I wish I had a syphon! If I had known all this was going to happen I would have gone to the grocer. Say When."

He said. But would to God he had accepted it neat!

For this was pre-war whisky, relic of the Reverend Thomas Metcalf's deep cellar, strong and smooth as silk. Fortunately she had obeyed his saying of When with instantaneous accuracy. One could see she was a drunkard's daughter and well trained.

"Personally I should never be surprised to wake up and find myself floating down the river—away and away! This is such a treacherous time of year, don't you think, and how one dislikes seeing swallows on telegraph wires! Do have another! To keep the cold out."

Yes, one could be uncommonly cosy here, listening to the river and the trees, hearing the oil-lamp purr (for sentiment's sake one might keep an oil-lamp and use it from time to time, though De Quincey evenings would demand candles), reflecting on one's deep-ensconced solitude. No one would come to stay in such a house as this. They could not. He would turn the second bedroom into a bathroom.

"I often wonder where I should get to. Out to sea, perhaps. But even in mid-Atlantic I should remember your kindness to my rabbits. Beverens, you know. I could not bear to eat them."

He glanced across the table. She also was keeping the cold out, and it had greatly improved her. Sister to the beauty of the young leaf is the beauty of the skeleton leaf, having the last skirmish of its vegetable blood before the winter sucks it into the mould. She had pulled off her sou'wester. Her cropped hair was white as thistledown, and when she laughed a wrinkle appeared on her long sheep's nose. But was this the last bottle of Mr. Metcalf's whisky, or would it be possible, possible . . . ? No doubt she was all filial piety, the daughters of abominable fathers always are; but five guineas would be more to her advantage, with five guineas she could light a roaring fire in that deserted Moloch's altar there.

"I see you are looking at that picture, Mr. Kinloch."

The walls of the room were plastered with things in frames, and he was not consciously looking at any of them. But now he followed the direction of her glance to the picture above the mantelpiece. It was a large steel-plate engraving, luridly brilliant. "Kermesse," perhaps, or possibly "Boors Carousing."

"It is a very fine specimen, I believe. And very valuable. My dear father thought the world of it." Leaning across the table, her light whiskyed breath on his cheek, she exclaimed: "Sometimes I think I will take it down! *But if I did,*" she said, "*what can I put in its place?*"

"Why need you put anything?"

"Oh, I must, I must! Because you see, if I took it down there would be the patch on the wallpaper. The different coloured patch where the wallpaper hasn't faded. It would always be there to remind me."

"True."

True, indeed. It would always be there to remind her. Absent or present, the boors would always be carousing. Morning, noon, and night Miss Metcalf would see those drunken grinning faces, those paunches and overturned flagons and wrinkled boots, those frank vomits and idiot rejoicings. Morning, noon, and night it would remind her of the Reverend Thomas Metcalf who had drunk himself to death and left her stupefied and penniless. Absent or present it would taunt her with an inherited alcoholism, a desperate maidenly desire for strong drink.

Even at this moment, overset by her confidence, she had begun to whimper and the first tears were rolling gaily down her flushed cheeks. In compassion and horror Adam Kinloch got up and made his hasty farewells.

Midway in the meadow he stopped and wrung his hands. The poor old wretch, the hapless elderly Iphigenia! Chance and the swollen river had brought her to his door, but only as another chance and the swollen river might have carried her past it. *Regrettable death of one of our oldest parishioners, Miss Metcalf, daughter of the late Revd. T. Metcalf, once Rector of Little Bidding. The deceased lady presumably fell into the river whilst attending to her rabbits, to which she was devoted. All those who knew her will feel her loss.*

All those who knew her! He began to walk on again, his hands in his pockets. All those who laughed at her, and hinted about her, and never went near her. There was nothing for it, he would have to pull himself together and be neighbourly to Miss Metcalf, take her for drives, ask her to tea, give her fur gloves at Christmas. Perhaps he could find a nice cheerful water-colour of some Welsh mountains to replace the "Boors Carousing." But really the kindest thing to do would be to walk down with a bottle from time to time and tipple with her. He would sit in her father's chair, and as the evening wore on, and the chairs creaked louder, she would scarcely distinguish him from the Reverend Thomas, all would be as it was, she would be a girl again, sipping from father's wonderful glass, and feeling proud to sit up so late like a grown woman. What a story she would make!

"You to the life!" he said aloud. "Do nothing for her, but put her into a story." The admission released him. He quickened his pace, he bounded up the steps to his door, he let himself in, he threw off his wet coat, he glanced at his wrist-watch. It was four o'clock. It was still raining. With a long sigh of relief he walked sedately into his library, sat down, and pulled a writing-pad towards him.

A Speaker from London

MRS. BENTON had always believed in showing consideration. Consideration for others cost so little and meant so much. Consistently practised, consideration for others became a habit and cost nothing at all. Now with the ease of habit she turned to the less-well-furred woman beside her and said:

"Dear Mrs. Mabberley, may I throw myself on your kindness? May my poor Miss Tomlinson—my secretary, you know—come in and warm herself at your fire while we are at the meeting? I really don't like to leave her in the car. The poor thing has had influenza and I'm afraid she got chilled to the bone dealing with that puncture."

Mrs. Mabberley, less accomplished in showing consideration than Mrs. Benton, replied that if Miss Tomlinson did not mind being left alone and sitting in the kitchen—"We haven't sufficient coal for two hearths," she concluded rather acidly.

"But of course! Who wouldn't love to sit in the kitchen? I always say this war has taught us to appreciate our kitchens. An Aga?"

"An Esse."

"Quite, quite perfect!" Mrs. Benton glanced at her

watch. "If you wouldn't mind showing us the way? Miss Tomlinson! Mrs. Mabberley says . . ."

Mrs. Mabberley said: "But wouldn't she really prefer to come to the Village Hall and hear you speak?"

"No, no! She has far too many opportunities to hear me speak. Besides, she's got a really terrible cough."

Mrs. Benton's tone of voice implied that not only had Miss Tomlinson many opportunities but that she slighted them.

With a last effort to safeguard her groceries Mrs. Mabberley said: "If you hear anyone moving about the house, Miss Tomlinson, don't be worried. It'll only be the Rector."

As the two ladies walked briskly towards the Village Hall Mrs. Benton observed: "I always feel that it's a little inconsiderate to ask my poor Miss Tomlinson to listen to my talks. After all, my message is really for Youth."

Mrs. Mabberley obliged with a titter. She also reflected that she was fifty—but a rector's wife must be eternally young. Mrs. Benton continued. "A poor thing, but mine own. And really, it's so difficult to get anything like a secretary nowadays that I'm thankful for her. I've had her Reserved."

Meanwhile Miss Tomlinson had taken off her hat and her gloves, wiped her glasses, which the change from an outdoor to an indoor climate had misted, sat down at the kitchen table, and pulled a pen and a wad of thin letter-paper from her bag. Turning over the pages already written she went on with her letter.

. . . *this everlasting war. Sometimes I wonder if you will even recognize me when we meet again. I expect I shall be sick. Something silly, anyhow, or it wouldn't be me. Perhaps we had better agree to carry a flower so as to know it's us. The price of flowers is awful. Two and six for a dozen snowdrops. But I have to buy them sometimes, all the same. I can't do without flowers, they make such a difference.*

She paused, and read, and added a mark of exclamation after the word "sick." Her pen trailed on the page. Suddenly she began to write again. *What a godsend! I have a whole hour to write in. Mrs. B. is doing her lecture, and thank God this time she has let me off. I coughed all the way here and it must have worked, anyway she has gone off, having graciously arranged that I should sit in the Organizer's kitchen. It's just the sort of kitchen you'd expect, with one of those posh cookers like a family vault, and everything so neat and hungry-looking it's enough to give one the creeps. When we have a kitchen we'll have a proper fire you can poke up, and blue and white china and a geranium on the window-sill, and a smell of bacon, and a cat. I wish there was a cat here, I could do with some company. But there's nothing but a rector, and he hasn't shown up yet. She mentioned, though, that he would be round and about. Just a gentle reminder that if I stole a currant I'd be heard doing it. What beasts these people are. The war means nothing to them.*

The spurt ended. She looked back over the written pages and numbered them. She had a typist's handwriting, hasty, irregular, and unformed. She herself resembled her handwriting; for her wearied middle age was yet callow and gawky, and the lines in her face had no maturity, they were as though some abrupt ageing process had seized and fixed the grimace of a schoolgirl.

She shivered, and coughed, and began to walk about the room to warm herself. Presently she discovered a battered *Good Housekeeping* tucked away beneath cookery books; and for a while she read it, and a look of melancholy greed appeared on her face. But it did not hold her long. She gave a conscious laugh, replaced it, and went back to her letter.

Slowly she wrote: *Sometimes I feel so blue, darling, I don't know what to do with myself. And then I hear Mrs. B. doing her bloody piece about how after all one has only to remember our brave men and our own small troubles seem such small things, don't they? And then she gives one of her wistful grins, and bears up even if her tea is late. The war means simply nothing to these people, simply a wonderful opportunity to be paid six hundred a year by the Government for going round telling kids what splendid fun they'll have being killed. Only now it's going down mines and scrubbing floors. I look at her and I think of you . . .*

The sound that had been the Rector on his prowls hardened into a light resolute tapping. There was a man looking at her through the window and smiling. As she rose he moved away and she heard his footsteps pause on a doorstep. She found her way to the back door and opened it.

"Good afternoon, Miss. Excuse me interrupting you"—he eyed her consideringly and went on—"but I saw you writing. I suppose you wouldn't care to buy a couple of pencils." He opened a case, pulled out pencils and blocks. "I've got thin paper too, air-mail stuff."

Sliding it into her hand he said: "You can take my word for it, a letter from home makes all the difference. You can't write too often. I know."

She looked at him.

"Seems queer to be doing this," he said, "after fighting in Africa."

"What?"

"It's just another hard luck story," he said dismissingly. He allowed enough silence and went on: "You wouldn't think it, would you, to look at me? And you wouldn't think it either, after all the speeches they make and the bits in the papers about heroes and all. But I was a Desert Rat all right, believe it or not. That's why I know what letters mean. You go on writing, my dear. And I hope he comes back luckier than I did."

"But . . ."

"Yes, I know. Where's my disability money and all that? Why am I on the road selling rotten pencils and job-lot paper?" He looked hard at her. "Bit of red tape got tied in the wrong sort of knot. That's why."

"Wait a minute," she said. "I'll be back in a minute."

Out of their kitchen store-cupboard she took tins of salmon, of meat, of treacle, of peaches, cartons of tea, slabs of chocolate, and packed them in a carrying-bag and remembered to add a tin-opener. As she worked she could hear him on the doorstep, shifting from foot to foot, and hurried to fill the bag and carry it to the door.

"I can't get at their whisky," she said. "It's locked up. But some of these things you could swop. Now go!"

He began to thank her, saying that he would never forget her, that the world was a queer place and maybe they'd meet again, that the chap who had her was a lucky one, that girls like her were what a man fights for.

"Go, go away!" she cried. "Go away before I begin to believe in you."

He went, and dived with gratitude into the church, where he repacked the stuff in his case. He might be able to get away with it, but she wouldn't. There would be hell let loose when it was discovered. At the bottom of the carrier there was a pound note, so she'd pinched the housekeeping money into the bargain. She must be one of those delinquents, he decided. A lot of them were leased out as servants, especially in places like rectories. Yes, that was it. A delinquent.

For some reason this conclusion eased his mind, and he quitted the church more comfortably than he had entered it.

Story of a Patron

SO BRIEF was Horace Rump's notoriety as a Genuine English Primitive that Mr. Haberdine who discovered him never received his due as a connoisseur. Mr. Rump was a retired policeman, the husband of the village postmistress, and a large pale man, mute as a mushroom. Mr. Haberdine was also retired but had no wife to obscure him from the public eye. He had retired from a business which traded on the London Stock Exchange, and some said he had been a passive agent in the process, the impulse for leisure and a quiet country life having been forced on him by circumstances. But no scandal touched him in Dogbury. He lived in a tidy house with a very tidy garden. He owned and carefully preserved a stretch of trout-stream. He was a churchwarden and went to church on every possible opportunity.

Mr. Rump went to church only at Christmas, at Easter, for Harvest Festival, and on the Sunday (a Sunday in Advent) which came closest to the date of his birthday. For some years he was no more to Mr. Haberdine than an impression of a tenor voice and a correct demeanour—an impression deepened on every occasion of Mr. Rump's attending public worship. Then, one

Easter morning, Mr. Rump approached his churchwarden and asked him if he had noticed that the jampot at the north corner of the font, containing daffodils, was an earthenware jampot.

Mr. Haberdine thanked Mr. Rump for drawing his attention to the lapse. He would see to it.

"Yes, Mr. Haberdine. Pray do. I have always understood that clear glass is permissible. Earthenware, no." Had Mr. Rump been speaking in the Court of Arches he could not have spoken with more authority. Mr. Haberdine thanked him again and told Mrs. Baggs, the church charwoman, to return the earthenware jampot to secular life.

A little while after, when Mr. Haberdine was buying stamps, Mr. Rump appeared from the parlour behind the post-office counter and said that if Mr. Haberdine had the time to step into the parlour he would like his opinion on a cactus. The cactus proved to be fine and fleshy, but only, it seemed, a pretext. Before it was an easel and on the easel a portrait of the plant, one of those portraits one sees in seedsmen's catalogues, irrefutably accurate and yet strongly laudatory.

"I didn't know you painted," said Mr. Haberdine. At the time he did not know, either, that he was a connoisseur.

"Being retired, I looked round for a little hobby," said Mr. Rump. "I don't and never have approved of idleness. Correspondingly, I took up art."

Mr. Haberdine asked to see more examples of Mr.

Rump's art, and Mr. Rump produced a portrait of Mrs. Rump. It was a remarkable likeness, quite as accurate as the portrait of the cactus but more dispassionate, as though Mrs. Rump had been grown by a rival seedsman. After praises, Mr. Rump brought out a larger canvas. " 'Harvest Festival,' " said he.

At first glance it was a still life of apples, tomatoes, beets, carrots, and a pumpkin, painted in the same seedsmanly spirit. But in the bottom left-hand corner was a minute clergyman (about half the size of a carrot), surpliced and on his knees—a very discriminating presentation of Mr. Aubrey, the rector. And emerging from the top right-hand corner was a Hand (much larger than the pumpkin), manicured and extended in a gesture of ownership. Mr. Haberdine examined the picture with pleasure. Its symbolism was immediately clear to him and the kind of symbolism he approved of. He asked Mr. Rump if he had ever seen an American film in which the Deity was represented in the same reverent manner. With the reserve of the artist Mr. Rump answered that he had not seen such a film.

These were all the canvases he would reveal. Later, he said, if Mr. Haberdine cared to step round, there might be more.

Mr. Haberdine went home in a fever of connoisseurship. It was a scoop, he told himself, already a patron of the arts, and then thought quickly, provided no one else gets hold of him! His impatience was great, but the feeling for negotiation which he had learned during his business career taught him not to show it. Outwardly calm, he waited for another summons from Mr. Rump. It came in just about a week.

The new picture was more animated than "Harvest Festival" but just as symbolical. A public-house was suspended like a phœnix in a bouquet of flames. Its windows showed a lighted interior where debauchees were revelling with cards and mugs under a clockface registering ten minutes after the official time of closing. At the summit of the composition, floating in a calm night sky, was a gigantic, highly articulated Ear.

Mr. Rump took Mr. Haberdine's encouragements calmly and said he had another piece in mind, to do with a funeral. This also took about a week and enforced the same teaching of the proportional relations of God and man. An Arm, draped in a dark blue sleeve, stretched across the centre of the canvas and along it went a funeral procession, iced with white flowers like a wedding cake. Beyond the blue cuff a Hand, stately and manicured as before, negligently let fall a manikin draped in a shroud.

Mr. Haberdine realized that in Mr. Rump he had found not only a natural but a reliable genius. He asked if anyone else had seen the pictures and was pleased to hear that Mr. Rump was keeping them to himself.

"Quite right, quite right! It would never do if they got into the wrong hands."

"They won't. There's no larceny where I'm about."

"But you would not mind an expert opinion? Just a

professional opinion, binding you to nothing. A valuation . . ."

"I don't need a valuation. I know their value right enough. Five pounds apiece, and I wouldn't take a penny less. Not that, either, unless they go where they'll be appreciated as they ought to be appreciated."

Agonized at the thought of some five-pound tourist chancing on his Unknown Master, Mr. Haberdine exhausted himself in persuasion. Finally, and on an understanding that Mr. Rump would be bound to nothing, he won permission to introduce an expert for a few minutes.

Leaving nothing to chance, Mr. Haberdine went to London on the breakfast train and spent nine pounds fifteen shillings and ninepence in entertaining Mr. Esme Bosworth-Griggs. Mr. Bosworth-Griggs was renowned for having a flair. He also excelled in what his friends called handling. So gifted a man was not to be wooed in a couple of sentences. Repeatedly Mr. Haberdine explained what a remarkable artist Mr. Rump was and how much more remarkable for being also a retired policeman. "Think of that Swiss fellow," said he. "Rousseau. Why shouldn't an Englishman do it too?"

Mr. Bosworth-Griggs did not answer this. He spoke of the intricate nature of art, the long apprenticeship that is needed to become a connoisseur, the enormous odds against spotting a winner. It would be hazardous too, he said, to stake much on putting over a name like Rump.

Mr. Haberdine said that Rump was no worse as a name than Botticelli, and easier to remember.

In tones warmed by whisky and old acquaintance, Mr. Bosworth-Griggs begged Mr. Haberdine to keep out of art."You'll only get overenthusiastic, Habbie, like you did that other time. Take a friendly tip and keep out of it."

"But these things have got more than art. Much more. They've got appeal. Think of the American market! Why, the first thing they notice about London is the police force."

"No, Habbie. Definitely no. Speaking as a friend, I can't in conscience go into it."

"Very well, then. I'll take it on alone."

Suddenly melting, Mr. Bosworth-Griggs said he would come down for a week-end's fishing.

It was a triumph for Mr. Haberdine.

Yet when the week-end came he began to wish the triumph unwon and Mr. Rump his undisputed darling. Though Mr. Bosworth-Griggs said little and made no promises, it was patent that his flair had told him that Mr. Rump would repay handling. "You must get him into the Church," he pronounced. "There's always room for a genuine religious artist. Simple faith, the eye of a child, calendars, and all that. I suppose he's reliable? Won't go off on vegetables?"

"Can't stop him if he does, can I?" inquired Mr. Haberdine pettishly. "Art's chancy—you said so yourself."

Mr. Bosworth-Griggs mused on. "It's a pity about his name. The Free Churches would never hear of a religious artist called Rump. It'll have to be those progressive chaps that go in for Socialism and processions and popery. Well, I'll have a look round. Meanwhile, you must nurse him."

Mr. Rump was a quiet nursling. Fed with paints and canvas, he produced a picture weekly, and except for an anxious interval when he went off on dogs, his productions continued to express simple faith and the eye of a child. In one respect his childishness was inconveniently more manifest than his faith. He was exceedingly secretive. Even when the Dean of Jude's came to inspect the new master he refused to exhibit more than three canvases and then only with the blinds down.

The Dean was Mr. Bosworth-Griggs' first catch. There could not be—so he wrote Mr. Haberdine—a better one. And he added that provided Mr. Haberdine steered clear of religion and put forth a good lunch, he could say pretty much what he liked, as the Dean was one of these Thomists.

Presently commissions began to come in: two banners, and a sign to hang outside a hostel. Mr. Rump took the first breaths of fame on an even keel and utilized his excursion into dogs for one of the banners, which was commissioned by a Guild of St. Bernard.

"But shouldn't it be the Saint?" ventured his patron. "I'm afraid it was the Saint they wanted."

"I paint what I know," replied the artist. "There's

the dog. There's God." He pointed to a monumental Leg encased in dark blue against which the dog, with a trustful expression, was leaning.

At this period Mr. Rump was still limiting himself to representing only sections of the Deity—sections always vast and smooth and, where flesh, of a rich, creamlike pallor, and, where covered, covered in dark blue. Sometimes the dark blue covering was embellished with silver full moons, and this convention was noted by Lady Cuthberta Wugley (a friend of the Dean's and, so far as a woman may be, a Thomist herself) as typical of Rump's stylization, which marked him a Genuine English Primitive. For by this time the name of Rump was on many cultured lips and spoken with confidence.

Throughout the autumn Mr. Rump went on producing, and on the second Sunday in Advent he went to church for his birthday. During the sermon Mr. Haberdine observed the artist gazing steadily and somewhat critically at a stained-glass window, and he was not much surprised when the next work of art, entitled with majestic plainness "The Almighty," turned out to be a full-length. This warranted a letter to Mr. Bosworth-Griggs, in the course of which, after mentioning that the new work was very fine and full of genuine English Primitive feeling, Mr. Haberdine ventured to query whether it was all right for the First Person of the Trinity to be clean-shaven.

Round about Christmas Mr. Bosworth-Griggs paid a second visit to Dogbury. Everything, he said, was coming on nicely, and he had hit on the right word for Mr. Rump's art. "Theo-realism! Links him up with Dali, you see, and yet shows why he's a step up. Now we've about got to the stage when we can discover him. The question is, who's to do it?"

"Didn't I?" cried Mr. Haberdine.

"Not advisable, dear Habbie. It really would not do. I did think of the Dean, but something's come over the Dean. He says he'll open an exhibition but that's as far as he'll go. There's that Wugley woman . . ."

"If you think I'm going to be elbowed out of this, you're mistaken!" exclaimed Mr. Haberdine.

"Dear boy! Nobody's elbowing you. I said fifty-fifty at the start, and . . ."

"I'm not talking about fifty-fifty. I'm talking about art. Who discovered Rump? I did! And I mean to have the credit of it."

"You can't, Haberdine. You'd sink it. You can't, unless you change your name."

"And what about Rump? You've got Rump to reckon with. Rump's a retired policeman, he knows the law, he isn't going to sit by and let himself be discovered by whoever you please to send!"

"Damn Rump! He's got nothing to do with it."

"*What?*"

Mr. Haberdine's yell expressed a genuine reverence for art. Mr. Bosworth-Griggs' quick ear recognized something new and incalculable. He gazed thoughtfully at Mr. Haberdine and said in a mild voice that quarrels between old friends were abhorrent to him and that for the present it would be best to postpone everything. Mr. Haberdine agreed.

That same evening Mr. Haberdine began to establish his copyright. He visited Mr. Rump and bought for five pounds the picture called "Harvest Festival." Then he posted a bill on the church notice-board announcing that a remarkable specimen of local talent was on show at his house. There would be an entrance fee of sixpence a head and the proceeds would go to the Church Roof Restoration Fund. Soon one pound nineteen shillings had been raised for the fund, and Mr. Haberdine was known everywhere in Dogbury as the man who had discovered Mr. Rump.

The artist took his fame very modestly. Indeed, there was something austere in the way he received congratulations and put by inquiries as to how much Mr. Haberdine had paid for the painting and whether the foremost carrot was taken from life. So reserved was he that he did not think fit to mention that another art lover had visited him, introducing himself as a friend of Lady Cuthberta Wugley's. So there was nothing to prepare Mr. Haberdine for the shock of receiving a card inviting him to the private view at the Damon Galleries of an exhibition of Theo-realistic paintings by Horace Rump. And as the card reached him only the evening before the date named he had little time for reproaches or inquiries.

Seated in the breakfast train, Mr. Haberdine was not

sure whether he was going to the Damon Galleries in order to demonstrate a disinterested love of art or to have it out there and then with Bosworth-Griggs—if indeed that serpent dared show himself. As for Mr. Rump's part in the outrage, he could not bear to think of it. To be diddled by a serpent was bad enough; to be deceived by a simple religious artist was beyond all.

The serpent was present, and came forward to greet him, and had the effrontery to set about introducing him as another of Rump's admirers. Blinded with rage Mr. Haberdine could hardly distinguish between the people he was introduced to, all of them speaking in art-loving tones and all of them, it seemed, established admirers of Rump and devotees of Theo-realism. As for the canvases, he could not look at them, so deeply was he chagrined at discovering how many of them, and those the gaudiest and most full-lengthed, he had never set eyes on. He did, however, recognize the Dean, whose slightly withdrawn manner and occasional coughs made it clear that he was keeping to his promise to introduce the new English Primitive.

"Quite a throng, isn't it? Quite a throng," said Mr. Bosworth-Griggs, bustling around and seeming to love everyone present—even, such was his audacity, Mr. Haberdine. "Excuse me, Avery. I'm sure I oughtn't to drag you from your prey, but I must just introduce my old friend Haberdine. He lives in the same village as Rump and knows him well." A man who had been going round the pictures with a prim conscientious face and whom Mr. Haberdine had assumed to be a gallery attendant or the picture framer or perhaps a private detective, turned at these words, and was therefore undoubtedly Timon Avery, the celebrated art critic. He now examined, with the same sad conscientiousness, Mr. Haberdine's quietly-patterned cravat.

"What sort of man is Rump? Does he lead a regular life?" he said.

"Oh yes, very."

"Hmm. Is he a religious man?"

"Oh yes. He goes to church."

"Hmm. Is he ever violent?"

"Never," replied Mr. Haberdine, surprised but confident.

"Hmm." Mr. Avery turned back to the pictures.

"He's enthralled by them," whispered Lady Cuthberta Wugley. "Look, he can't leave them."

That was quite true. Even when the Dean moved to the centre of the room, as to a pulpit; even when everyone else became fixed and hushed and gazed with determination at some chance object, as though they were members of a congregation; even when the Dean proclaimed that he had been asked to say a few words, Timon Avery continued to mouse among the pictures, staring with the sad, pale eyes of a cat preoccupied with some private consideration.

The Dean spoke as a Thomist should, displaying a heavenly intelligence armoured in knowledge of the world, and for exactly five minutes. He explained the necessity for Theo-realism, and how the development of Europe's finest thinking called for it, and how Horace Rump had answered the call. He also explained how fitting it was that the European demand should be answered by an Englishman who had served his country as a guardian of law and order and how the guardianship of law and order would be prevenient to the grasp of theological conceptions. He then bade those present observe the acumen of Mr. Rump's simple formulæ and compared the somewhat repetitive quality of the pictures to the sameness of the solar system. Penultimately he acknowledged himself obliged to the artist for a deepened insight into the Nicene Creed. Finally he announced that it would give him pleasure to introduce Mr. Rump to this first gathering of his admirers and called on him to come forward.

Mr. Rump came forward, emerging from behind a heavy curtain. He wore a dark blue suit and looked even smoother and more clean-shaved than usual. His pale face was inscrutably composed. He did not bow, speak, or offer any indications of being human. Under his arm he held a canvas, and this he suddenly thrust into the hands of the Dean, using that gentleman as an impromptu easel.

"My latest," he said, speaking at last. "Portrait of myself."

There was, with model and painting thus juxtaposed, no doubt of it. Though the style of the picture was timeless and the dark blue suit disassociated from any mere tailoring by a hierarchic severity and symmetry, the portrait was of Mr. Rump. It was also, even to the silver-moon police-uniform buttons, an exact facsimile of all the other portraits around the room, portraits, according to Mr. Rump and the Dean, of the Almighty.

Folding his arms, wrapped in schizophrenic calm, Mr. Rump stood surveying the first gathering of his admirers, surveying them with the authority of the Creator examining the creation and not yet absolutely convinced that it was good.

The admirers, glancing from Mr. Rump to Mr. Rump's Theo-realistic works, stood silent and confused. Only the Dean, obscured behind the self-portrait, displayed no realization that something awkward was taking place. Only Timon Avery, slipping away like the serpent from Eden, seemed at peace with himself and the world.

Unknown to History

I WAS brought up not to stare about me in other people's houses but to present an appearance at least of being more interested in my hosts than in their mantelpiece ornaments. But when I enter Miss Hurry's drawing-room I can—indeed I must—abandon this classical style of behaviour. Everything in Miss Hurry's drawing-room—and there is a great deal—is in some way connected with Miss Hurry's family, and not to observe a newcomer there is to be guilty of slighting a cousin, a cousin removed, or a great-great-uncle. This time my politely riveted gaze brought an introduction to three water-colour sketches.

"Nina's," said Miss Hurry. "But I suppose you don't remember Nina."

The water-colours were very blue, mountains in the background, flowers in the foreground, animals among the flowers. Each was signed firmly across the bottom left-hand corner, "Nina Prothero, 1888."

"Alps," I said, since I could not claim to remember Nina.

"Maritimes," said Miss Hurry. "Do you notice the animals? So like Nina. She was devoted to animals.

That's why she got so excited, that time we were all in Paris."

I settled myself in tranquil expectation.

"It was in '88. I had come out the year before and Nina and Mary had taken me to Paris. They were my mother's cousins and like aunts to me. Roger was there too. In those days ladies didn't go to Paris alone."

"Was Roger like an uncle?" I asked.

"He was considerably younger than Nina and Mary. Quieter too. The men on that side of the family are usually quieter than the women. We were all living in Paris near the Bois, and soaking in the atmosphere. We used to read *Le Matin*. One morning there was a most extraordinary article in it, and as it was raining Roger began to read it aloud. It was about the Black Mass. I suppose when you were nineteen a Black Mass was nothing to you?"

"I expect I'd heard of it anyway."

"I hadn't," said Miss Hurry. "And really Roger should have left it alone, for it was quite unsuitable, apart from its effect on Nina. However, he didn't, though he rued it afterwards. The article was by a Paris journalist. He was called on by a heavily veiled lady, and went with her to a grand house in a lonely street. There she took him into a room that was furnished like a chapel—a Roman Catholic chapel, of course, dear, hung with black velvet and very badly lit. But he did manage to see that at the farther end of the room there was some sort of altar. And sitting on the altar was a large goat. A live goat.

"And Mary Prothero said, '*Pas devant l'enfant.*' Which of course was ridiculous, considering we were all living in Paris. But Nina said, 'Go on, Roger.' So he went on.

"They lit candles all round the goat and waved incense about. There was quite a large congregation, mostly ladies, very well dressed and fashionable. Suddenly all the ladies tore their clothes off and rushed to the altar. Of course the language, the language of the article, made it all seem much more abandoned and passionate, and the ladies much more undressed. French does, doesn't it?"

"It does indeed."

"But at that moment Nina sprang to her feet and snatched *Le Matin* from Roger's hand and danced on it. Then she began to talk about letters to *The Times* and going to see the Consul."

"She was shocked, I suppose?"

"Shocked, my dear? She was frantic. Because of the goat, you see. Nina could not tolerate cruelty to animals. And while Mary was saying that it showed what French society was like underneath, and Roger was saying it was probably all made up, and I was saying nothing, Nina was asking us to put ourselves in the goat's place, to imagine what it would be like, if one were a goat, to be compelled to sit on an altar being singed with candles and suffocated with incense and rushed at by women with no clothes on. Then Roger most unfortunately said that the journalist said nothing about the goat seeming to mind it. Nina said at once, the poor creature must have been drugged, no better than a circus. Nina could not bear the idea of anything being drugged, lions, babies, Indian widows, it was all one to her. And before we could do anything she had thrown on her hat and darted into her gloves, and was gone.

"Roger went after her. She went straight to the office of *Le Matin* in a cab and asked for the address of the journalist. She got right in to the editor, talking about the goat and scandals and clothes being torn off. The editor drew Roger on one side and asked him if the journalist had insulted Madame, and became very chivalrous and confidential, and Roger realized that he was on the brink of having a duel arranged for him."

"The editor was not interested in animals?"

"Roger thought he hadn't quite understood. Nina's French, you see, was very fluent, especially when she was excited, and hard for a Frenchman to understand. And she kept on referring to the goat as *la pauvre petite*, and saying that she had never been so outraged. Anyhow, when Roger explained that he never fought duels the editor lost interest and said with the greatest politeness that he must go out to lunch.

"So next Nina found a police-station and began all over again, telling the police that they must trace the journalist in order to trace the goat. They were more attentive than the editor of *Le Matin* but they didn't really understand either. Just as they seemed to be grasping what Nina meant and dipping their pens in their inkpots she went off at a tangent about her dear old Baphomet (Baphomet was a goat the Protheros had when they were children, dear, I'm sure you've never heard of him), and apparently that gave them an impression that Nina was saying it was a shame her goat couldn't have a Black Mass too. And they became so odd and suspicious that Roger had to drag Nina away.

"So he was bringing her home, and quietening her with the British Consul, when they happened to pass a church. He saw a wild light come into Nina's eye, and she flew into the church and fell on her knees in front of a confession-box. And Roger heard her say, *Mon père, je suis Protestant.* She must have been thinking of Jane Eyre because, in fact, if Nina was anything she was a Rationalist. But there she was, pouring it all out in loud whispers. And Roger could do nothing, only wander round looking at the poor's boxes and saying to himself, 'The Seal of the Confessional.' Poor Roger! It was all made rather worse for him by Nina's hat. You see, the Protheros were Anglo-Indians, particularly Nina and Mary, and whenever they travelled they dressed as if for the tropics. Bonnets were very small just then, but Nina wore an immense mushroom hat with a veil floating from it, and a dust-cloak. And this made her noticeable, except in the Jardin des Plantes, where she might pass as a Mahometan. But of course she couldn't be taken there, because of the animals. So Roger said quietly that he thought Nina would get on better without him, he was only a red herring and a handicap to her.

"So Nina and Mary went together, in their dust-cloaks, to the British Consul. It turned out that he had been at Winchester with Pomery Prothero, but otherwise he was not helpful. He seemed to think that Nina should leave it alone. Of course he didn't know Nina.

"Mary soon gave up, but Nina went on and on, inquiring for the goat or else for the journalist, and talking rather unwisely, I'm afraid. For Roger told me in confidence that an acquaintance of his, a very nice quiet Frenchman, had asked him out to dine and very nicely and tactfully had suggested that Roger should restrain Nina in case she precipitated an incident. Roger asked, 'What sort of incident, a fall of the Ministry?' But the Frenchman said, 'No, it was more serious than that. Nina might be mistaken for an agent of the Freemasons.' Roger assured him that Nina always dressed like that, no power on earth could get her into a bonnet. After that the Frenchman said no more.

"And then, two days later, Nina did not come back to lunch. We waited and waited. No Nina. Of course Mary and I could not help remembering that poor woman—all quite untrue, I believe—who developed cholera on the eve of the opening of the Paris Exhibition and was spirited away by the police, nothing left of her at all, and a general with whiskers in her bedroom, and the daughter went mad. Really so silly of us!—for just then a messenger boy brought us a note from Nina, and a lovely bunch of flowers, sent from the Gare de Lyon, saying that she had met a delightful artist, a fellow-spirit, who was leaving that afternoon to paint the Maritime Alps. And Nina had decided to go too, and was too busy buying paints and nightgowns to come back to lunch.

"Oh, how thankful we were! Nina had given up the goat, that was all we thought of. We were quite accustomed to Nina acting suddenly, and there is always the Crédit Lyonnais, so we did not worry at all. Of course it never occurred to us that the artist was anything but a lady artist. Mary was rather upset when Nina came back a fortnight later with a great many water-colours and quantities of local pottery and a string bag full of oranges and egg-plants, all carried by a very polite young man in very wide trousers. We knew that nothing could have happened except water-colours. Still, at that date one wasn't supposed to be so much carried away by love of art."

Miss Hurry lit a cigarette.

"Did you see much more of him, that artist?"

"No, dear. He seemed to fade away. Anyhow, Nina had become a vegetarian by then which was why she brought so many oranges."

He faded away, that devoted and persuasive young man. So vanish good spirits, their mission ended. But whether he returned to private life or to the ranks of the *Sécurité* I have not yet been able to make up my mind.

Sweethearts and Wives

SOMETIMES Justina and Midge discussed what would happen if all their husbands came on leave together. Lettice could go to her grandmother's—but then William would not see her, and really she was now a nice displayable baby. The Sheridans might find a double bed at the farm—but that would not take away Roy and the twins and if Mrs. Sheridan slept out one could not expect her to be back in time to get breakfast. Justina and Tom might have a little honeymoon at The Griffin—but that, as Midge said, would break up the household.

Without husbands the household consisted of three women and four children. Justina, who liked figures, had worked out that the average age of the party was thirteen. If one left out Mrs. Sheridan, who was over thirty, the average age fell to eight years and nine months; but to leave out Mrs. Sheridan except arithmetically was inconceivable, for Mrs. Sheridan was the king-post and glory of the establishment: she cooked.

Both Justina and Midge had married early in 1940. To their respective mothers it seemed natural, since both husbands were in the forces, that they should stay on at home, keeping their spirits up, poor little things, by giving a helping hand in country houses suddenly denuded of servants and enlarged by such creative activities as organizing First Aid Points, entertaining Polish officers, and breeding table rabbits. When they decided to set up house together in Badger Cottage it seemed hopefully probable that the poor darlings would soon tire of cooking for themselves—the more so as Badger Cottage was such a disadvantageous dwelling, lonely, ugly, derelict, miles from any shop and all the water needing to be pumped by hand. But the discovery of Mrs. Sheridan quenched this hope. Mrs. Sheridan was also married to a fighting man; he had been a circus hand, now he was in the R.A.S.C. Mrs. Sheridan, bombed out of Mitcham, had come to Suffolk to find a home for herself, her three children, her Alsatian dog, and her horse. The horse had associations, Mrs. Sheridan could not bear to be parted from it; the billeting officer had washed his hands of her when a fight between the Alsatian and Justina's two poodles elicited the fact that Mrs. Sheridan would do anything and everything for whoever made a kind home for her and her beautiful Shirley. Midge's baby immunized her from conscription, but the poodles could not do the same for Justina, who had been conscripted to replace an auctioneer's clerk in the local town. By privily dismembering her bicycle, hiding its fragments in a fox-covert, and declaring it as stolen, she was in a position to claim Shirley as an essential means of transport. The horse thereby received a ration, Mrs. Sheridan was able to live with them and be their cook, and when the Alsatian was reconciled to the poodles the compound household worked perfectly.

Another of Mrs. Sheridan's beauties was her farmer friend, Mr. Cuffey. Until Shirley had become an essential means of transport he had kept her going with oats, and he still stabled her. For Mr. Cuffey (though a grimly married man who had never been out of Suffolk in his life, and regularly taking the collection at a Methodist Chapel) had a romantic streak in his nature which made him the slave of Mrs. Sheridan's black eyes, purple velveteen trousers, and *haute école* graces. At dusk Mr. Cuffey would materialize to woo Mrs. Sheridan with illegal cream and extra butter, and sometimes a nice little bit of pork and sometimes a pheasant which had been foolish enough to get itself entangled in a rabbit snare; and having a generous circus-like outlook on windfalls Mrs. Sheridan would share these courtesies with Midge and Lettice and Justina.

Arriving on the heels of his telegram Midge's William found himself being conducted, as it were, for a tour through the Sheridans: Mrs. Sheridan, Pamela, Gloria, and Roy Sheridan, Driver Sheridan (by proxy of photographs and such a wonderful likeness to the boy), the Alsatian, and the horse. But unfortunately he had come on a day which was not the morrow of one of Mr. Cuffey's more impassioned dusks.

"If only we had known you were coming we could

have feasted you on the wages of sin," remarked Midge. "As it is, it must be fish."

"I expect William gets a lot of fish in the navy," said Justina. "I expect he's sick of fish. Midge, come outside one minute."

William heard some serious murmurings, and the sound of damp flat objects being turned over. Then they reappeared.

"Darling, I'm afraid it won't be fish after all. You see, Justina brought back what she could get, and what she could get was one largish sole and a plaice. And we were to share the sole and Mrs. Sheridan was to have the plaice. She prefers plaice. But the sole isn't big enough for three, and if we had the plaice too, there would be no fish for Mrs. Sheridan. So we think she had better have the sole and we'll have toasted cheese."

Justina said: "Fortunately there's quite a lot of cheese."

"My only criticism is, that you don't seem to have accounted for the plaice," said William.

"Oh, Mrs. Sheridan will have it for her breakfast."

"She likes plaice, she likes it better than sole," Midge said. "It would be a shame to deprive her of her plaice."

"Especially as she has been so obliging about the sole," added Justina.

At breakfast (tea, toast, apple jelly, and the smell of Mrs. Sheridan's plaice), and at intervals during the rest of his leave, William Corby reminded himself that it is ridiculous to think much about food, that by virtue of his profession he was better fed than any civilian, that it was very handsome of Mrs. Sheridan to share the wages of sin with his daughter as well as with her own children, and that it was marvellous for his Midge to have a cook. If she had not got a cook, Midge explained, she would never have time to make so much jam. Midge's jams seemed to be the mainstay of every meal; though this, as Midge also explained, was partly because if you made jam without as much sugar as the book said, it had to be eaten down immediately or it mildewed. On Sunday too, he got a little riding, as Mrs. Sheridan lent him her horse.

"But oughtn't she to have a rest?"

"My Shirley is a professional horse. She's never missed a performance, bless her!" said Mrs. Sheridan, who, as it was Saturday evening, had an agreeable odour of gin about her.

The Alsatian and the two poodles came along too, and killed and ate several rabbits. Justina's Tom, so he had heard, was a good shot. Every man, thought William, at any rate every husband, should be able to shoot; and he reproached himself that he was incapable of shooting anything except stationary bottles at fairs. One is not a good shot unless one can shoot something edible. He would like to meet Tom Debenham and have some shooting lessons. It would be fun if Tom's next leave should coincide with a leave of his own. It might mitigate this disquieting impression of having four children at Badger Cottage, and two, or possibly three, wives. Yet democracy is desirable, we must all aim at a future of more equality and less formality, and the household at Badger Cottage was a step towards such a future. It was probably reactionary of him to dislike seeing so much of Mrs. Sheridan's purple trousers and never feeling sure whether it was Lettice wearing Pamela's rompers or Gloria clasping Lettice's teddy bear who needed picking out of the pond. If he had spent the last three years at home instead of at sea he would be better at recognizing his own child. Meanwhile he was riding Mrs. Sheridan's horse, and Lettice and Midge were sharing in Mr. Cuffey's love-gifts, and the joint households of early Soviet days must have been more ill assorted and infinitely hungrier.

These reflections were cut short by the necessity of galloping across a field in order to deter the two poodles from pulling down a sheep. The fact that the Alsatian had taken no part in this assault but was virtuously engaged in hunting another rabbit was a further reminder that it is the more privileged classes who have most to learn in the matter of citizenship.

Badger Cottage was going on much as usual when a parcel came for Midge containing a large tin of olives and a note from William hoping that they might come in handy. As going on much as usual meant just then that Roy and Lettice had whooping cough and that Gloria had eaten the greater part of an indelible pencil, Midge remarked that dear William must be at Gibraltar, didn't Justina think, and the tin of olives was put by in the store-cupboard. Midge was too loyal to voice the wish that William had sent tinned salmon instead, Justina was too polite to say so either, and Mrs. Sheridan only said: "Well, thank God it's in a tin anyway. Which reminds me, Midgie, my twins have got at the jam you put up in the attic, at first I thought it was mice but it's too sticky for mice."

It might have been expected that Tom, coming on leave so soon after this, would have eaten the olives. William had allowed for it. Besides having heard that Tom was a good shot, he had heard that Tom was something of an epicure; and he had said to himself a trifle wistfully: "To each according to his need"—being, as his father-in-law said, a damn sight too well up in all that anti-God sort of stuff. Tom did not eat the olives because after his first meal during which Gloria sat on his knee, toyed with his hair, and addressed him with purple lips as Daddy, he announced that he was going to take Justina to London to see some shows and have her nails cleaned.

Driver Sheridan, on the other hand, entered at once into the spirit of Badger Cottage, arriving with a goose, twenty-four kippers, several tins of army stew, two bottles of whisky, four hundred cigarettes, six yellow dusters, and an invaluable collection of nails, screws, bolts, and washers, the property of H. M. Government. During his stay he undertook a number of repairs and improvements, mended the meat-safe, washed and clipped the poodles, lifted the main-crop potatoes several weeks too early, repainted the dog kennel and part of the front door, hung a swing for the children, fixed an aerial to the wireless, and did things to the pump. On his last evening too, he further asserted himself as a practical man by fighting Mr. Cuffey, spending the remaining hours alternately beating and embracing Mrs. Sheridan. Bruised and admiring she passed the next day wandering among his incompleted works, saying dreamily: "There'll be something to show for this, I shouldn't be surprised."

The first perceptible aftermath of Driver Sheridan, however, was the cessation of cream and butter, and Mr. Cuffey's inability to go on stabling Shirley, never in all his days had he known such a messy horse. It is difficult to place a full-sized horse with delicate lungs; circus life, as Mrs. Sheridan explained, the draughts playing on open pores, always weakens the lungs, think of monkeys. Finally Shirley was accommodated at the Vicarage, where the sound of the organ, said Mrs. Sheridan, would be like old times to her. Justina more moodily remarked that she would now be more than a mile from her essential means of transport, and that the Transoms would henceforth expect a regular supply of prizes for their incessant Church Roof Restoration Fund whist-drives—as was indeed the case.

Other tokens of Driver Sheridan's manliness were still lying around when William came on his next leave: festering heaps of wood and wire that needed only a few finishing touches to become a rabbit-hutch, rusty bolts and cog-wheels which should have been put back in the mangle but somehow got overlooked, and several fresh neuroses in the pump.

"Come just when you're wanted," said Mrs. Sheridan warmly. "You sailor-men are always so handy."

If he had not been so obliteratingly in love with his wife William Corby would have remembered to arrive as a good provider. As it was, he just got into the first train with nothing more than love, lemons, silk stocking, presents for the children, and good intentions. The presents for the children were eaten in a flash, the stockings were put away, love is always impalpable, one cannot live on lemons—he did as best he could with the good intentions. There was certainly a great deal to do. It seemed to him that Badger Cottage was much dirtier and more disarrayed than the passage of six months and the transit of Driver Sheridan could justify. But then, as he told himself, he came off a ship, a childless, melancholy world of its own. Four children would no doubt make a destroyer look as tousled as Badger Cottage; and he thrust down the inward retort to this, that children on a destroyer would be kept in better order and cleaned at regular intervals.

Women, he also told himself, are less fussy than men; it is a wise natural provision to fit them for the inevitable mess and confusion of maternity. Women, too, are braver, more adaptable, probably hardier, certainly less self-indulgent. They are more primitive and so better attuned to the primitive state of the universe when, as the Scriptures so acutely remark, the earth was without form or void and the waters brooded on the face of the earth: which reminded him he must try to do something about the bathroom. But the brave, adaptable, hardy, self-disciplined, and primitive Midge had spots on her chin, moaned in her sleep, and smoked more than was good for her. As for Justina, she had a cold in her head. It was so violent that she did not go to work, so instead Mrs. Sheridan rode into town and did the shopping. Mrs. Sheridan was a somewhat erratic shopper but she always remembered the children; and it was so nice for her, Midge pointed out, to be reunited with Shirley. To give Mrs. Sheridan more time to enjoy this reunion, Justina cooked. Justina had been taught cooking at a domestic college for young ladies. She knew how to make omelettes, fudge, several kinds of soufflé, coffee, and—theoretically—soap. Unfortunately omelettes and soufflés cannot be made without breaking real eggs, so Justina's home-lore chiefly expressed itself in coffee. For the rest there was always cheese, and Midge's jams, and the national loaf, now so vitaminous that it was almost as ready to ferment as the jams. Why on earth, thought William, didn't I have at least the foresight to bring them some ships' bread? Busy himself as he might in being a man about the house, his thoughts dwelt increasingly on food. But he did not realize how enchained he was to sensual lures till the message came from Mrs. Transom to say that after all she could not have them to supper as the vicar had just gone down with mumps.

"Mumps! Oh, my God," wailed Midge. "None of them have had mumps! Oh, Justina, why did we let them go to the Children's Service?"

Mumps, thought William. I've had mumps. I could perfectly well have gone to that supper.

"I expect he was in his pulpit all the time," replied Justina. "It isn't as if he'd been confirming them or christening them. And somebody had to go to church after they'd been so obliging about Mrs. Sheridan's horse."

Damn Mrs. Sheridan, thought William.

"What's mumps?" asked Mrs. Sheridan, and answered herself by adding that mumps were all in the day's work. She could afford to be philosophical, thought William, she had not lost a supper, she had been staying at home anyway to look after the children. Which, of course, was very good of her.

Justina remarked that there was still quite a lot of the beetroot soup left. Midge said she didn't wonder. William didn't wonder either.

"And there is any amount of oatmeal. Isn't there something called brose that's made of oatmeal—with cabbage in it? Didn't Robert Burns sup brose?"

Mrs. Sheridan opined that there was more than that in Robbie Burns's brose.

"What a pity we gave the remains of the rabbit to the dogs!"

The word "olives" began to shape itself in William's mind, but he said nothing.

"It's the very devil," mused Midge, "feeding the dogs. They're much fussier than the children. Or us."

"They don't appreciate the war, poor things," said Mrs. Sheridan.

"Do you think a jam roly-poly? That would be filling. And we must browse down that elderberry jam that wouldn't set."

The word "olives" now thundered in William's brain. His tongue was swollen with keeping silence. Some flash of his electrical agony must have reached Justina, for suddenly her face became illumined with intellect and she said: "I know! I've got it! We'll open that tin of olives that William sent us."

"Oh, Justina, we can't! It's gone."

"Gone? Have those blasted children . . ."

"No, it's not the children this time. It's me. I gave it to the Transoms for a whist-drive prize."

She spoke to Justina exactly as the conventional wife confesses to her husband that she has given his trousers to the jumble sale. Amid everything else he was feeling, William was able to notice this.

"Damn! What on earth came over you? No one in this village would know what to do with an olive."

"But you don't like them, Justina. I'm not all that fond of them, really. And Zoe doesn't like them either, for I asked her."

"I can eat them," said Mrs. Sheridan. "But that's not to say I actually enjoy it."

Midge lit another cigarette. She was still looking like a guilty wife and spoke savagely. "What else could I do, Justina? You know how those blackmailing Transoms hound us for their whist-drives. It's all very well for you, you are out all day, you don't know much about real life. But I can assure you, what with thinking about food for the dogs, and washing for the children, and prizes for the Transoms, real life isn't worth living!"

The ensuing silence was broken by Roy Sheridan who strolled in carrying a tin chamber-pot in which there were some baby mice. He had found the mice in Daddy's rabbit-hutch, he explained. There had been lots more, but they had got away. Now could he have some cotton-wool to make a nest for them? Presently William was able to suggest that, since they could not sup at the Vicarage (where at this moment, he said to himself, those Transoms were devouring olives like quails and manna), they should walk the four miles into town and have dinner at The Griffin and try for a bottle of whisky for Justina's cold, that is, if Mrs. Sheridan would stand by her generous offer to keep an eye on the children. It was a lovely frosty night, the walk would be fun.

"We shall get up our appetites," he concluded.

Mrs. Sheridan was quite ready to stay at home, so William set out with his two wives.

The dinner and the whisky cost in all four pounds seventeen shillings. Both Midge and Justina got slightly drunk and were much improved by it. In fact, it might have been called a successful evening if it had not been riddled by a tendency to remember Mrs. Sheridan and feel how unselfish she was and what a pity it was that she had been left out of it.

The House with the Lilacs

IT WAS in 1937, when they had been settled in their house for over a twelvemonth, had outgrown its first charms and found new ones and were no longer pained by its demerits, that Mrs. Finch, speaking as if she had given the matter long consideration and at last felt justified in announcing her conclusions, said that sometimes she rather wished they had bought the house with the lilacs, after all.

"Which house with lilacs, mother? We looked at dozens. Do you mean the one with the condemned well?"

"No, dear. The house with the lilacs, with the lilacs. You remember. It was a white house with a slate roof. We saw it on that very stormy day, and the wind blew a lilac bough against my hat and drenched me. It was the proper lilac, the kind the Turks sent to Vienna."

"Where was this house?"

"Down a long lane."

"Yes, but *where?* What county was it in?"

"Now how can you expect *me* to know that?" She looked at her husband with interest. "Anyone would think, Henry, that we were spending a week-end at

Brighton instead of sitting here with our well-grown family."

"Why do you wish we had bought that house instead of this? Was it nicer?" This was from Arden, the Finches' twelve-year-old son who was going to be a mathematical genius.

"I don't know that it was nicer. But it had some queer funny ways that one would have grown very fond of. I liked that old laundry with the stone floor and the round-topped windows and the fig-tree growing all along outside. Do you remember? On one side of that bricked yard where there was a grindstone under a sort of thatched canopy."

"Did the grindstone go with the house?"

"Oh, certainly! That was one of the things I liked, there were so many oddments that went with the house. The yellow pony-cart and the melon-pits and the churn and those thousands of flowerpots in the shed and the bottle-tree."

"Bottle-tree, mother?"

"You know. You've constantly seen bottle-trees—like an iron diagram of a Christmas tree, with spikes in tiers all the way round it, and you put empty bottles on the spikes."

"But why?"

"Order and tidiness, my child."

"I can't remember the house at all," said Cordelia. Clara could not remember it either. No one could remember a house with anything like a bottle-tree standing in a bricked yard where stood also a grindstone under a sort of thatched canopy.

"Isn't it extraordinary," said Mrs. Finch, gazing at them as if they were Northern Lights. "And yet you might be living there at this moment!"

As a conversationalist Mrs. Finch was considered hard to follow. Not that she was obscure, she was clear as the cuckoo; but, like the cuckoo, it was hard to follow her for one could never be sure into what tree she had flown. Thus it is likely that many of her references to the house with the lilacs went unrecognized, being taken as overtones to measles at the Rectory or death among the bantams; but some statements were categorical. Among the noteworthy aspects of the house with the lilacs was a mulberry tree with a little lawn all to itself, a long-tailed piano in an attic (Mrs. Finch herself had thought this rather odd and had wondered how it had got there), a case of stuffed owls in a linen-cupboard, a little wire staircase (well, iron, if you must be so circumstantial) that went up through the bathroom, and the weathercock, which was a fish.

"I am surprised that you don't remember the fish. Don't you remember the old gentleman telling us that in the gale of 1929 it was blown into a pond?"

"What old gentleman?"

"The old gentleman who lived there with his two sisters. Just as it might be you, Arden, with Cordelia and Clara. One of them was stone-deaf and the other wore very large dark spectacles. They were so congenial, and I was so sorry for them for having to leave their house."

"Why were they leaving it?"

"They were going to Bulgaria to look after their roses. They lived on attar. I mean it was their income. Not humming-birds. Of course that explained the house being so full of icons and why, when I saw those owls in the linen-cupboard, I supposed for a moment it was the Holy Family."

"How much did they want for it?"

"Ten thousand. Yes, Henry, I remember you looked like that at the time. Or was it three? Whatever it was, it gave you exactly that legal expression."

Nothing likelier, thought Mr. Finch, than that he should be wearing a legal expression, since he felt so uncomfortably as if he had been cross-examining a Welsh witness. It would have been a relief to his mind if he could have found Elinor out in a lie. But she was distressingly consistent; though there seemed to be no end to her recollections of the house with the lilacs, each as it came dovetailed into the whole with a Mozartean purity. The time of year, the day's weather, the dimensions of the house—every unity was preserved. Apricots never appeared among the lilacs, not a mulberry dropped, the wind still blew from the south, the house continued to face southeast, and the soil remained a light loam. This unshakable consistency (one cannot call it cunning) is one of the qualities that distinguish the person with a delusion from the ordinary liar. In his anxiety to convince himself that Elinor was just ordinarily lying, he asked more and more questions; and every question's answer made her seem more resplendently the soul of truth, more transparently the vehicle of what Cordelia called an obsession and Clara referred to as a Thing. To Cordelia and Clara, normal well-brought-up girls of their date and station, there was nothing disconcerting in their mother's showing signs of madness; it was what their lessons in psychology and physiology had taught them to expect. Arden was too young or too mathematical to mind whether his mother was going mad or telling lies, he just liked hearing about the house. If Arden would not ask so many questions, thought Mr. Finch, ten to one the whole thing would die away and be forgotten. What was quite out of the question was that the house with the lilacs should exist and have been inspected. It was asking too much to suppose that he and his two daughters, all three of them perfectly in their senses, should have unitedly mislaid every recollection of the bottle-tree, the long-tailed piano in the attic, the two asparagus beds, the bathroom traversed by a little wire staircase, the icons in every room, and the owners who were leaving this unique property for a rose farm in Bulgaria.

Meanwhile he must hope that all this would blow over, and that so much evocation of a non-existent house would not unsettle Elinor from the house they were in. It had been trouble enough to decide on it, and now if all those months of journeys in hope and dubious returnings, desks littered with house-agents' hyperboles, keys that didn't fit, punctures in unfrequented by-roads, halts to inquire the way from deaf old women and people who were strangers there themselves, were to go for nothing! However, Elinor did not seem to be growing unsettled, continuing to live in the real and describe the unreal and be none the worse for it.

In the following summer she sprained her ankle, but in a quite rational way, falling off a ladder while picking morello cherries. Her exclamation too—"Now I can really give my mind to learning the harp!"—was not more eccentric than her usual run of aspirations. Doting on his Elinor in her infirmity (like most husbands, Mr. Finch released a peculiar tenderness towards a wife in physical distress), he drove to the county town to see if he could buy a harp, and took his daughters with him as he did not wish to look like a fool. They could not find a harp, but the disappointment to Mrs. Finch was mitigated by two facts: that she had not realized what they had gone to town for, vaguely supposing that it was something to do with a fishpond; and that during their absence she had made a new friend, a young man on a walking tour who had called at the house to ask for a drink of water.

"And isn't it delightful?" she said. "Mr. Doubrov knows the house with the lilacs. He stayed there when he was a child. He remembers everything."

"It was my godfather's," said Mr. Doubrov. "He is quite shortly dead." He offered this information as though he were handing his hostess a bouquet. Emitting smiles of tender enthusiasm, he was clearly another of the numerous young men whom Mrs. Finch turned the heads of.

"Mr. Doubrov was there in July, so he did not see the lilacs. But he ate mulberries and wood-strawberries, and was taken for drives in the pony-cart, and he remembers a wooden summerhouse, which must have fallen to bits, for it wasn't there when we saw the garden. While he was there the house was struck by lightning."

Mr. Finch, Cordelia and Clara variously muttered, "How interesting," and "How delightful," and stole hangdog glances at each other. Mr. Finch, in addition, wiped his forehead with his handkerchief.

"Where was this house?" said Cordelia.

"It was on the land. It was altogether on the land. No other houses were there."

"Down that very long lane," said Mrs. Finch confirmingly. "But when Mr. Doubrov was there the piano was downstairs, in the room with the French windows and the big bird-cage."

"But in what part of England, Mr. Doubrov? You see, though my mother remembers the house so well, she can't remember what county it was in. None of us can, as it happens."

Mr. Doubrov raised his very black eyebrows and looked sorrowful.

"Ah! Now that I cannot say. I was a stranger, you see. A child. We went by a train from London. We got out. We drove. My mother said to me, 'Look, what fields! Like parks!' Then was I sick. But where was all this, I cannot tell you."

Sensitive enough to feel that something disastrous had got loose, Mr. Doubrov turned with a reassuring look to the only person who felt no need of reassurance, and said, bowing from the waist: "If in my tour I shall find this house again, Madame, it will be my pleasure to send you the photograph."

The Way Back

"AND on the first of July," he said, "I landed in England. And that is the end of my story. If it had not been for my parents," he added, "I would have stayed in France. In France or in Europe. Somewhere around. You can pick up nationalities off the roadside, any nationality you please, on the roads of Europe today. If I could have been reported Dead I would have stayed, people soon get over a death. But Prisoner and Missing is the devil; my parents would have gone on worrying. So I came back."

As they walked out of the restaurant he said: "Do you think I've changed?"

"A great deal," she answered. "Your nose is more hooked, your whole physiognomy is changed. You look formidable. It's very becoming."

Now he began to survey the traffic going westward through the town. The driver of a lorry slowed down and drew in to the edge of the pavement.

"Like a lift, soldier?"

"Bridgewater," he said, "or thereabouts."

"Take you as far as Somerton."

"That'll do nicely. For while I'm waiting for my medical," he said, turning to his companion, "I'm putting in time hiking about to all the places I've been a misfit in. To find out if it was them or me. Well, good-bye. Thanks a lot for finding me changed."

A week at home, she thought, was as much as he could stand.

The brewery, the gasworks, the outlying bungalows, were behind them, and the fat and flourishing landscape imposed its contours on the course of the road. The driver asked: "Been back long, soldier?"

"Fortnight tomorrow."

"Germany?"

"Poland, actually."

"Quite a step," said the driver. "How did you get there? Do you smoke?"

The cigarette was smoked out between Caubourg and Alençon, for to begin with the driver asked questions and imposed glosses from other narratives. Ash-trees and hedgerow elms, unimpaired steeples, buildings trim or sagging under nothing more than senility, flowed towards them, whisked by, were demolished behind them. It was easier to tell his story thus than while sitting in a restaurant eating stewed rabbit. Food should be eaten in silence anyway, with the savage attention which is its due.

The narrative travelled eastward, was noosed to a standstill, was released and went eastward again, lost its impetus, halted, and turned back.

"Pity you couldn't get as far as Moscow," said the driver. "But I dare say you'll get there some time.

Seems to me if I'd been behind barbed wire and got out again I'd never settle down for long. I'd be afraid to. Shouldn't think you feel altogether like settling down, not at your age."

"As long as they don't settle me down in some base. —Well, thanks for the lift."

"Thanks for the story," said the driver. "Best of luck, I'm sure. Meet you in High Street, China, eh?" He drove off, the engine noises whacking his empty ears. Oughtn't to dump him in a base, he thought. A week of the old spit and polish would be as much as he could stand.

This time it took him longer to pick up a ride, or he was harder to please. Two private cars paused to invite him but he waved them on, saying that he was not going their way. Finally he got into a builder's lorry which was travelling in the same direction. This time he kept his story to himself. Yes, he was just back. No, he had been a prisoner. Yes, it was all right being home. He sat and stared at the oncoming road. The landscape had flattened out, its contours were less imposing, the road seemed able to assert its independence and take a straight course. Where it crossed a muddy little river, shuffling along under willow-trees, he halted the driver.

"Going to the camp, are you? Well, you'll see some changes since last time."

"I can see them from here," he replied.

The crest of the last low hill was covered with hutments, hutments sprawled down its flank. They were painted over with a camouflage in tones of stale mustard. But under the milky sunlight of the day the mustard colours suggested some low form of animal life rather than any kind of vegetation. It was as though the hill were covered with a plague of caterpillars, caterpillars which since he had last been here had pullulated a thousand-fold. As a distant window tilted towards the sunlight, as a glass-panelled door opened or shut, minute flecks of light flashed out, and it was as though the caterpillars were slightly squirming.

He gave it a long steady look and then struck off across the meadow, walking on the raised bank of the stream. Even now, in mid-July, with meadow-sweet in bloom and dragon-flies hawking over the surface of the water, the rushes along the embankment were fastened together with wisps of muddied grass, the tide-mark of the winter's floods. The air had a particular smell, wild and pure, the smell of air unbound from the usual tether of hedgerow. As far as he could see before him there were no hedges. Ranks of willows, embanked ditches, sometimes a wire fence, marked the divisions of the land. He was back once more, walking freely where three years before he had walked furtively and defiantly, defending in the teeth of a carefree communal life his personal right to be solitary and full of cares. He was back once more, and the mood of those days rose up and reclothed him, so that he found himself suddenly and intently quickening to forgotten preoccupations, so that the downward sighing of a willow-bough became his loathing of a red face adjusting itself to a mouthful of beef, so that a hairy plaster of mud on a post where cows rubbed themselves became his conviction that when he made his first drop a fly would be drawn into his windpipe and he would land ignominiously stifling.

Now he could see the farm quite clearly, a small composed building of earth-coloured brick with a hooded porch and a round window above it. It had an air of being tranquilly idle, of sitting with its hands folded among the rabble of barns and sheds and ricks and cow-stalls that surrounded it. As one came nearer the illusion of idleness was lost, the house rang like any other farm-house, with noises of feet, buckets, children, and crockery. From here it sat with its hands folded, watching the pears ripen on the south wall. But now the charm was lost. It no longer bothered his mind as it had done then and afterwards in thoughts and in dreams.

He skirted around it. Something else was missing too, something that had been an irritation, a fret. The dog, of course. The dog that had always barked was not barking. Just as he was thinking with pleasure that it must be dead—it had been a most objectionable, unhappy cur, always tied to its kennel, always working itself into hysterics—he caught sight of it, still tied and with the same dirty enamelled bowl still beside it. But this time it was not barking. He shrugged his shoulders and smiled and walked on. One brings back something from one's travels, if only the ability to best an old watch-dog on a chain.

Ahead of him in a field alongside the familiar track, some men were gathering in the remnants of a crop of rushy hay. He could see the flies round their heads, fetched by the smell of their sweat. He turned off to avoid them. In this sea-level landscape with its foam of meadow-sweet, its banks of green willow rippling and tumbling like some real wave thrust up through the sea-level earth, one could walk at random and yet never lose one's bearings. The last time he walked here he had tried, most deliberately tried, to lose himself. But in vain. A group of poplars, a cattle-shed, a detail of the horizon, a gated bridge across a drain—there was always something to whistle him back. It would be difficult to be lost even in the whole of England, England is so small; what hope of getting lost on Sedgemoor?—unless one is poor Monmouth.

Monmouth's men had fought with pikes, with clubs, with scythes. In 1940 pikes were issued to the Home Guard, and all the old fire-eating gentlemen went round saying that the pike is a damn fine weapon, sir, and a match for any automatic. Cold steel, sir . . . Unfortunately Monmouth's men had not found it so. Yet their tactics had been good, taking advantage of the terrain and its morning mists, tying up the royal troops in rheins and ditches. The mistake had been to engage in battle—a mistake generals are particularly prone to, and Monmouth had been Captain General of the King's Forces, enough to ruin any commander. With Maquis methods, a long smouldering insurrection might have changed the story of England; though sabotage is not so effective against an enemy who moves on foot and horseback, not by train and lorry, who depends on local industries and not on power-stations. Yet the moral effect, the unsettlement, the demoralization, would have been as great, perhaps even greater; for using the superstitions of the times . . . And here again he was riding off on the same fallacy, giving King Monmouth's men the mentality of three centuries later, whereas, in fact, they would have been just as much subject to haunts and witches as their adversaries.

The aspect of a group of willows told him that by inadvertence he had at last achieved his ambition and was lost. Then he saw a man with a gun come out from among them. In an instant he was flat on the ground, refuging his human-coloured face and hands behind a tussock of grass. Life rushed into him, he was alive again and devoted, mind, body, and soul, to living. Lying motionless, his ear to the ground, his muscles striking the brilliant bargain between immobility and the power to leap to his feet in a flash, he felt himself changed from lead into gold.

The man's foot took a step forward. There was a twang, the twang of a single-strand wire fence. A rabbit got up beside him, flicked its ears and ambled towards the sound. There was a crack of gunfire, and he heard the pellets scatter and bounce on the dry ground and the drumming of the rabbit's feet as it galloped off, and the man's slow voice saying: "Missed 'un."

So now he lay still because he had made a fool of himself, and heard the man walk away, pause and shoot again and walk on. A bad shot, he had not got his rabbit this time either. At last he got up and dusted himself and beat off some ants and looked about him. The group of willows was still strange; but a puff of wind blew the boughs to one side and through them he saw on the southward skyline the camp in its mustard-coloured camouflage, sprawling and faintly squirming. He was not in the least lost. He had walked in a circle, that was all.

"And I thought I had learned not to do that," he chided himself as he walked on to meet the main-road and his next lift.

Major Brice and Mrs. Conway

IN MAY 1946 Major Brice of the U.S. Army, revisiting London and liking it no better than before, drove himself into the country on a vernal impulse to re-examine a Mrs. Conway who in 1944 had been briefly his hostess and his mistress—and more to his taste in the second category. Her house had been cold, her bathroom had been gaunt, her table had been ill spread except when he spread it, and from sundown to sunrise he had been pestered with black-out regulations. That was how he had discovered her more satisfactory aspect. For while he lay reading in bed, the only place where he could escape from the draughts, she had burst into his room, wearing, of all things, a steel helmet—she had been out on some civilian nonsense or other—and saying furiously that if he was afraid to go to sleep in the dark he might at least exert himself to draw his curtains properly. As one throws a cover over canaries when they make too much noise he had switched off the light while she was still in mid-career. "Oh!" she had said, startled into primness. A minute later she and her helmet were scattered on his bed.

And really, that was the thing he most warmly remembered: her startled "Oh!" so inadequate and female, her lips, fresh with the outdoor cold, and the genuine satisfaction of having silenced them.

That was in February or early March. Ten days later he had gone off to a battle-school and after that to battle itself. "Give my regards," he had said, "to your English spring." Every dreary acquaintance of hers and her incessant sister-in-law incessantly had remarked to him that really he should see Ludworth in an English spring.

Now, as the lanes became familiar and the names he had known by ordnance map and hearsay appeared on the fingerposts—Abbot's Woolcombe, Little Poakers, Chelbury Regis—he was seeing it. There was too much of it, he thought, and all of it too close. Hawthorn hedges blocked his way like snowdrifts, the small steep pastures were bruisingly vivid with buttercups, and when he paused to study yet another fingerpost at yet another junction of floral rat-runs, the noise of the birds was deafening as musketry, and the smell of the May blossom made him sneeze. She had been much the same, he thought: her lust too lusty, her abandonment without sensibility; and all, like this landscape, in such a small way; for there had been no perspective of love between them, no basic tenderness, scarcely a farewell and no letter-writing. She had bestowed herself as the English sell bread: unwrapped, and unanalyzed.

As the house came into sight he thought: Perhaps she is away; and the surmise was followed by a distinct sense of relief. He wanted her to be away. But for all that he drove in between the stone gateposts and got out, leaving his bag in the car, and rang the bell.

The door was open, he could see into the house. It was as shabby as ever, so shabby that one could not see that it was two years the shabbier. After a while, since no one answered the bell (no one had ever answered any bell, for the only house-servant was stone-deaf), he walked in and went into the sitting-room.

Nothing was changed but everything was different. Presently he saw why. The hearth on which she had kept so inadequate a fire was blazing with sprays of beech and laburnum, with white irises and fat crimson peony blossoms. The faded green walls, the sheep-faced family portraits, the exhausted upholstery, were shadows in a garden; for trophies of flowers were everywhere, and through the open windows the branches which had rapped with wintry fingers on the pane extended into the room, mock-orange and clematis and sagging roses.

Except for the birds yelling outside all was silent. When he could bear it no longer he turned on the wireless. Out came a talk on the cuckoo. He twiddled until he found some dance-music, and made it as loud as possible. That always used to fetch her, then.

It fetched her now. She went by outside the window, wearing a blue dress. He whistled her. She made an almost imperceptible turn of the head, but did not pause.

When she had not come in he began to feel somehow alarmed. He switched off the wireless and heard her steps go swiftly along the passage. Then a door shut. That was all. He snapped on the wireless again, and the small action transmuted his feeling of alarm into anger and resentment. This was their English hospitality!

Unheard, she was in the room, wearing a green dress and saying: "Do you mind if I turn this down a bit?" just as she used to do. Then she turned it off, just as she used to do, and advanced on him with her ugly inattentive smile, the smile of a street urchin and not a woman's smile at all, and held out her hand, and said: "Hallo! How nice to see you."

Her voice expressed nothing beyond being in her own house and addressing someone who had entered it. But for all that she had stayed to change her dress. Her hand was quitting his when he took a firmer hold of it and kissed it. It was pretty much like kissing a lizard, a lizard with some ill-fitting rings on.

"Are you over here for long? Do sit down and tell me all your adventures. Did you enjoy the war?"

Aching to slap her face he settled back in a chair, crossed his legs, lit a cigar, and said: "Well, it was interesting. I suppose it would have been even more interesting if one had known it was in the nature of a last performance."

"Do you think so?"

"Well, there aren't going to be any more wars like that. All that's a back number, now."

"Oh, of course. You're thinking of your new bomb."

"I'm not the only one who's doing that."

"And do you know all about it, Terence?"

"No. We don't let it out quite as freely as that."

"What a shame! Never mind, perhaps you'll be allowed to drop one. On London, for instance. You'd love that."

"I mightn't feel too badly about it," he said. "But I wouldn't be doing it anyway. They'll probably come over by rocket."

"Better and better," she said. "Why, in the next war you Americans won't need to put yourselves out at all."

"No. We'll just be sending you parcels—as usual."

He looked at her green dress. It was ugly, made of a poor stuff and coloured with a poor dye. She had looked better in the blue one. Being a man of thoughtful character he reflected: Suppose she went and changed into an uglier dress because of me? If she imagined it enhanced her green eyes, she was wrong. It put them out.

"As a matter of fact," he said, "I just came down to look at the village church."

She laughed. "Suppose you have some tea first."

"Oh, tea!" But because she had laughed and for a moment had looked easy, he added: "Well, I'd like to eat another of those things like sponges. Crumpets."

"But one doesn't eat crumpets in May!"

She spoke with no more malice than a schoolteacher, and nothing she had said before was comparable as an insult.

"Of course not, of course not! It's their mating season."

She waited a moment or two and said smoothly: "You're looking very well, Terence. Did you come over by air or on a food-ship?"

He threw his cigar at the peonies and got up, just in time to see her walk into the room wearing a blue dress.

"Mary, this is Major Brice. This is my daughter, Terence."

Mary Conway was not a beauty, she had no style, she had nothing beyond the temporary advantage of being twenty years younger than the mother she so exactly resembled. So why should Ruth Conway sound so jubilant about her? She could not, she could not possibly know of his mind's slight misadventure with a blue dress.

"Major Brice has come down from London to see the church, darling. He hadn't time to see it when he was quartered here in 1944."

"I suppose you were frightfully busy?"

"Frightfully."

Twenty years ago Ruth Conway was just as obtuse, no doubt. But now, he reflected, she wasn't. Such a situation had possibilities.

"After tea you must show it to him."

"Oh yes, I'd love to. Do you like architecture, Major Brice?"

"I'm fascinated by your British architecture."

"He's seeing all he can in the time," remarked her mother.

"I suppose you are going back quite soon?"

"We Americans are always in a hurry, you know. We haven't got your background, we haven't got your sense of repose."

She turned to her mother and said: "Would you like me to do anything about hurrying tea?"

"Don't think about tea," he said. "I know how things are over here. I'd hate to take the jam sandwiches out of your mouths. It's just the church I want to see."

"Make sure he signs the visitor's book, Mary."

"I'm crazy about your old village churches. We have no churches in the States, you know."

"I expect you come from the Middle West," said the girl. "You ought to visit New England. There are some very nice churches in New England. They are made of wood and painted white, and they look exactly as if Sir Christopher Wren had designed some really grand bathing-machines for Queen Anne. They can be moved about on rollers too, which is more than you can say for churches here. You really ought to go to New England if you are so fond of churches."

"Don't the New Englanders speak with quite an accent?" asked the son of Vermont.

"Yes, they do, rather. It's supposed to be an English accent really. In some of the backward places in Lincolnshire the old people still talk like that."

"Your mother didn't tell me you'd visited our country."

"I was sent there in 1940 to be out of the way. I was there for two years and I came home with a collection of the wildest hats and such an accent that Daddy sent me to school all over again to be scraped."

With a picture in his mind's eye of how Ruth Conway must be enjoying herself he glanced round to confirm it. She was kneeling before the hearth. So she had knelt before, puffing at the fire with a pair of wheezy bellows and sometimes even dimly apologizing for the absence of central heating; but now she was tranquilly re-arranging her peonies. His week-end bag, he remembered, was still in his car. He was in two minds whether or no it shouldn't remain there.

Rosie Flounders

TEN years before she had been "that nice child, Rose Peverel," the long-legged, fair-haired, flat-faced daughter of a decaying family, who had been confirmed, finished in France, presented at Court, given a Sealyham terrier and a pearl necklace, and could reasonably be expected to marry. Marry she did, before reason expected it; and the widowed Mrs. Peverel was saying, with scarcely an adjustment of her maternal manner: "Flounders. Isn't it an extraordinary name? Midlands, you know. Of course he is almost twice her age. But they adore each other."

The business of twice her age was one of Mrs. Peverel's little adjustments. Roderic Flounders was thirty-two at the time of the marriage. But he had pouches under his eyes and a bulbous nose, he was going bald, and he coughed. It was kinder and better (Mrs. Peverel would go a long way in pursuit of kindness and betterment) to attribute these dilapidations to the hand of time. As a man of forty Roderic Flounders made quite a personable son-in-law, especially if one put an emphasis on the Midlands, where a higher standard of living and a harsher climate might easily bring pouches under the eyes.

To her intimates Mrs. Peverel allowed herself to say: "Provided he makes my little girl happy!" But this insurance against possible divorce proceedings proved unnecessary. Roderic made Mrs. Peverel's little girl extremely happy and clung to her as devoutly as though she were his better leg. Like many rakes, Roderic was timid and oppressed with fears and hypochondrias; his Rosie, with very indistinct notions of what they were all about, knew instinctively how to manage them. She was capable and confident and took a high moral line with his duns and a low moral line with his failings; she knew when to be rowdy and when to be clinging, and was, as one says, the making of him.

In return, Roderic was the making of his wife. He made her from Rose into Rosie. But how much she was Rosie did not manifest itself until the war.

When war broke out Roderic found himself in the army, in the R.A.S.C. The opportunities for smoking and drinking afforded by field-days had made him an enthusiastic member of the O.T.C. at his public school, and a general association of army life and days out had later carried him into the Territorials. With the notion that in times of war a wife is best disposed of with her mother, Roderic sold the lease of the house in the Midlands and Rosie and her small boy and his nursery governess came back to Mrs. Peverel.

There for two years Rosie was perfectly miserable. Her maternal feelings had been concentrated on Roderic, who really needed them; she could not deflect them to her child, who did not need them as he had his Miss Potter anyway and now had a grandmother. Her filial feelings, mislaid during her thrilling and rewarding married life, could not be refurbished into currency; and though Mrs. Peverel, still pursuing kindness and betterment, continually inquired if it wasn't wonderful for her to have her Rose back again, the question was merely rhetorical, since it was obvious to all who heard it that what she had got was Rosie Flounders and no rose of her own growing. Whenever Roderic came on leave Rosie begged and implored to be allowed to get away into some whole-time job, and Roderic, tickled to his heart's root by being begged and implored by his Rosie, replied that his peace of mind depended on her staying where she was.

Conscription could not rescue her, as she had the child; but when the Ministry of Labour decided that Master Flounders did not need the attentions of a resident nursery governess and a resident mother, and called up the nursery governess, Rosie saw her chance. Taking the same high moral line which had been employed on Roderic's duns in the delightful past, she now found that her conscience would not allow her to see poor Miss Potter, who was such a quiet gentle girl and really knew nothing of human nature, exposed to the hazards of a militarized world. All they wanted was a woman, any woman would do; and she would offer herself in Miss Potter's place. In vain did Mrs. Peverel invoke the name of Roderic. Roderic was in the Far

East, Rosie could do what she liked with him. Accordingly she made him into a hybrid of Saint George and Don Juan, and was positive that Roderic, who knew almost too well what life was really like, would never consent to the virgin tribute of Miss Potter. Mother and daughter fought briskly for a week, and were pretty well matched; for both were adept liars and perfectly indifferent as to what became of Miss Potter. Then Mrs. Peverel weakened—realizing perhaps that if she managed to keep Rosie she might get more than she bargained for—and agreed to the exchange, provided her little girl did not accept a job that would take her right away from her child. "Sleep in," said Rosie with the coarseness of the chaste; and came back from the Labour Exchange with the news that she had been directed into victualling and would work locally as a van-driver.

Rosie learned about van-driving from a veteran called Wangles. In his younger days Wangles had been an actor; he still retained a great deal of Shakespearian deportment, a stately gait and diction, an affability which made him an ornament to any bar, a warm heart, and a dispassionate outlook on the sacred rights of property. "Who steals my purse, steals trash," he would say, handing a bottle of whisky to a friend with that outward chest-expanding movement of the arm which on the stage represents a noble disposition.

Van-driving agreed with Rosie. Mrs. Peverel's handling of the alcohol shortage was aggrieved and unenterprising; Rosie was thirstier than she knew. She grew buxom and merry, and her face discarded the likeness to Mrs. Peverel which had been settling down on it. Besides getting enough to drink Rosie was sexually at ease. Her new friends having discovered that she preferred to be chaste, left it at that; she could romp and joke and be confidential without incurring any further obligation to bitch about, an obligation imposed on her and her like in their natural habitat by the claims of patriotism, international good-relations, or *quid pro quo* for Spam and stockings. There is a kind of simplicity which in sheltered surroundings thickens into stupidity but which being exposed to a naughty world develops into the positive quality of innocence. I watched this happening with Rosie. No doubt Roderic had begun the process. But respectability had conditioned and limited the good work; the path might be devious, but respectability was the destination, where the duns, finally disheartened, would cease from troubling and a crude past would mellow into knowing what's what and providing a sound qualification for being made a Justice of the Peace. Rosie's new friends thought no more of respectability than if they lived in the Golden Age. They stole and tricked and trafficked with the serenity of kittens, and were enjoyably high-minded into the bargain. I recollect saying rather sternly to Rosie that though I was by no means averse to a bottle of gin I was unwilling to pay the black-market price for it. Black market! said Rosie, she wouldn't touch the thing. Controlled price and take it or leave it was her motto. It was a fine motto, I said, but I could not see how it could be worth Rosie's while. Rosie said I need not worry, from time to time things happened to happen that way, windfalls, so to speak: but as for black market . . . Maid Marian in merry Sherwood could not have looked more beamingly self-righteous.

Having found me so congenially moral, Rosie felt, I suppose, that she could trust me. A friendship sprang up between us, one of those war-time friendships, open-hearted and dated as Morning Glories. When we met in the course of duty she would give me the latest news of what she called Roderic's Bottom Drawer. Roderic's Bottom Drawer had begun with the usual drinks and tobacco, but as Rosie got about more (they thought very highly of her driving) and made new contacts, the Bottom Drawer enlarged its scope and Rosie soared from mere acquisitiveness into connoisseurship. In January 1944, I remember, when the roads were like black glass and traffic almost at a standstill, she drove to Birmingham with her trousers lined with rabbits, on the hearsay of some full-length pure silk socks. Wangles, who was cultured, drew her attention to antiques and personally contributed a sixteenth-century Bible which he had come across in a shamefully neglected pew, bare ruined choirs, so to speak.

I don't know whether it was the Bible or the barometer, but the next time I met Rosie she asked me if I knew of any haunted houses knocking around. It appeared that she had conceived the fantastic ambition of finding a house for Roderic to come back to; and the incurably romantic Wangles was confident that the use of a flash-lamp coupled with some apt hootings and howlings would flood the market with haunted houses at bargain prices. Rosie's own idea of bribing a house-agent was quite as nonsensical. Eagles do not mate with daws; and if the whole contents of Roderic's Bottom Drawer had been offered it would have been about as compelling as a daisy-chain. But she had set her heart on it; nothing I could say would convince her of the majesty and grandeur of the house racket.

Then one day she asked me if I knew of a place called Upshott Lodge. It seemed a curiously artificial question. Everyone in the county knew of Upshott Lodge and its inhabitants, Miss Perdew, Peter Perdew, and Mrs. Lecheminant. They were the three remaining children of old Dr. Perdew, one of England's celebrated flogging educationalists. He had left the house to Miss Perdew, who was semi-idiotic, and for many years she had lived there with a companion, harmlessly enough. When the companion killed herself, Mrs. Lecheminant, who was commonly supposed to have eaten Mr. Lecheminant, came to live with the old lady, and soon after that Brother Peter joined them. Mrs. Lecheminant combined crazy avarice with visions. Peter was simpler—he was an elderly satyr.

I said to Rosie that I did indeed know of Upshott

Lodge and hoped that fire from heaven might fall and consume it and those who lived in it. Rosie said she hoped not, as she was moving there in a day or two.

Getting her foot in, she explained. After all, there was nothing wrong with the house, was there? I asked if Wangles was going too, to body out Mrs. Lecheminant's visions by hooting. Rosie said he might come along later, it all depended. Again she remarked that there was nothing wrong with the house. I agreed that it had a roof on it, and presently Rosie began to tell all.

She had heard on a side-wind that the old women believed, quite erroneously, that they were about to be served with a billeting order from the local Housing Committee requiring them to give up some of their superfluous rooms to a homeless family. So Wangles, accompanied by a lady of his acquaintance and seven small children (names, said Rosie, no matter), had spent a Sunday forenoon ostentatiously staring at the house, pointing to the smokeless chimneys and the bleared windows and using all his dramatic gifts to make it clear to Mrs. Lecheminant behind her curtains that he was a man and a father and likely to stop at nothing. Having allowed time for Wangles to sink in, Rosie had called at Upshott Lodge and suggested herself as a lodger. At first the sisters had shilly-shallied; but Peter had been favourable, and Peter had done the trick.

I said this was what I should have expected of Peter. Rosie laughed (she had a singularly pretty laugh—I would like to hear it again). Peter, she said, was going to be invaluable. Peter was going to run upstairs after her and die in a fit, like my uncle the Canon who died in a bawdy-house.

I knew it was waste of time to explain once more to Rosie that this legendary figure of the Anglican Church was not my uncle. In Rosie's world you do not know of legendary figures. You only know relations. I said that if Rosie were going to Upshott Lodge in order to put an end to Peter it was public-spirited of her, but that she would still have his two sisters between her and a vacant possession. Rosie looked at me with that blasting scorn with which people in provincial society ultimately look on people, however otherwise tolerable, from outside it.

"Do you mean to say," she said, "you don't know about the annuity? All the money they have is sunk in an annuity, and it is in Peter's name because he is the youngest. If Peter runs upstairs once too often they won't have a penny. They go, I stay. That's how I get the house."

No morality beamed from Rosie now. She looked as plain as a hen and as practical. The Higher Racket had called her into its service.

Presently she invited me to walk out to Upshott Lodge and have a look at it. We walked through the slums at the northern end of the town and left their barking dogs and slamming doors behind, and came to Upshott Lodge, squatting in the water-meadows.

I have never seen a more malignantly ugly house. It was Builder's Gothic, with inhumanly large windows, and plastered with every kind of cusp and knob and crocket. We stood in the dusk and studied it while a cold dry wind chattered among the laurels. One of its windows blinked wearily into illumination, and by the light of an oil-lamp (Mrs. Lecheminant could tolerate no arithmetic but her own, she would not have electricity because the meter might cheat) we saw Miss Perdew begin to hitch herself about the room brandishing a fly-swot. Rosie remarked that she would be much more comfortable in the Infirmary.

This continued to be Rosie's opinion. It was outrageous, she said, the way that Sister Blanche and Brother Peter made their octogenarian do all the household drudgery. They even rang the bell for her if they wanted anything, and the idiot would wander from empty room to empty room, peering round doors and saying: "Are you here, dear? No. You're not." Blanche, said Rosie, when she wasn't locking up the fish-bones, sat waiting to catch a glimpse of Papa and sometimes doing so very convincingly. That was how she kept Peter in order. One glimpse of Papa and Peter went down like a soufflé. I said that this might distract Peter from dying after the fashion of my uncle the Canon. That was where Wangles would come in, Rosie replied; one day Blanche would herself catch a glimpse of Papa that would astonish her. If I cared to be around on Wednesday evening I too might catch a glimpse of

Papa. Then she said that if I would be there keeping my ears open for P. C. Gull on his rounds, I could be a godsend, for Wangles, once he had got his teeth into Hamlet's ghost, would be deaf and blind to everything but his art, and the best way to warn him would be with half a brick.

For three months Rosie had not heard from Roderic. I suppose this was one reason why I agreed to be there. Rosie, scheming so heartlessly, hoping so childishly, to get a house for a husband who might never need it, was the kind of thing which gets under one's rationality and bites one.

Certainly I have never seen a crazier spectacle than Wangles. He had got himself up for the occasion with a mortar-board hat, a black gown, and long phosphorescent whiskers. He wore plimsolls, he carried an umbrella, he looked like something got up for the village flower-show; and till he began to make noises I despaired of him. Pacing to and fro on the long-haired lawn he coughed—a short, condemnatory cough. He made it sound thoughtful and rather hungry, and he did not do it too often. The enormous bow-window was hung with old-fashioned venetian blinds, the lamp-light escaped at the sides in a weak glow. Presently I saw a chink of horizontal light; the slat of a blind had lifted slightly, warily, like the eyelid of somebody shamming dead.

Wangles saw it too. He slid into the cover of the shrubbery. The silence was rent by a torrent of wild girlish giggles which hurried themselves into hysterical notes of ecstaticized terror and died away in a nightmare nightingale *jug-jug-jug-tereu.* Presently the late Dr. Perdew reappeared from the shrubbery and paced up and down, just as before, coughing. But this time the slats of the venetian blind were a chink open.

Between the coughs I heard poor old Wangles puffing and blowing. His falsetto was impeccable, but time will tell, and he was out of breath. If it weren't for those idiot whiskers, I thought . . . for shaken by the power of Wangles' reconstruction of family life in the old God-fearing days, I felt the need to pull myself together with a little impartial criticism. If it were not for those whiskers . . . and yet, as they mooned through the darkness, and the coughs stirred them, there was something to be said for them. Then I heard a door close very quietly, and round the corner of the house came Mrs. Lecheminant, padding and peering. Wangles was almost at the end of his yonderly pacing, in a moment he would turn about and confront the faint light from the northwestern sky, and there would be the devil to pay. There was a half-brick in my hand, as arranged, and I threw it at Wangles. But I am a bad shot. The brick hit Mrs. Lecheminant, and she dropped. I cannot honestly say I was sorry, but I was considerably perturbed. I was nearer being sorry when I saw the old woman lift herself on to her hands and knees and wait a little, and then, with a dreadful meekness, scramble to her feet and walk back to the house without a word.

Wangles had come round by the bushes untrimming himself on the way; now he stood at my side and said: "She thought the old gentleman had clipped her one." We went off together and had a drink at The Pure Drop, to keep the cold out.

I was so far called to the Higher Racket that when I saw Rosie two days later my first inquiry was whether Peter had found an opportunity to follow my uncle upstairs. Rosie said that he had, but hadn't died. She looked badly, and I found myself doing what I never supposed I would do: advising her to go back to her mother. Rosie said that boat was burned. Mrs. Peverel, after declaring that if Rosie disgraced her by living at Upshott Lodge she would be unable to look her friends in the face, had implemented the words by letting her house furnished at a superlative rent and retiring with her grandson and Miss Potter to a hotel at Lyme Regis. I suggested that Rosie should share my lodgings or try the Y.W.C.A. She replied as I expected. I did not ask her if she had heard from Roderic. It was plain that she hadn't.

Probably I did not persuade very skilfully; indeed I can't have, or I should not have suggested the Y.W.C.A. I was just going down with influenza. Influenza is an absorbing disease; I was so much taken up with mine that I forgot to notice that Rosie did not keep her promise of coming to tell me how things were going. When I got up, it was a Sunday, I thought about Rosie and decided that I would go and see her. It was the time of year people call Saint Martin's Summer. The first autumn gales were over, the air had a moderate conviviality, like China tea, everything was clean-rinsed, the unleaving trees had a look of independence and vitality. I was glad to be out, and at the end of my walk I found myself considering Upshott Lodge with a kind of hopefulness. It was as ugly as ever, but I saw its ugliness in the guise of the grotesque, and its woolly evergreens and conifers looked warm and sturdy. If Rose got it, I thought, and got Roderic, and they did it up and mowed the lawn and were happy in it, the poor wretch of a house might yet know a serene and comical old age.

I rang the bell. It was one of those pull-down bells that answer from the depths of the house long after one has pulled—like dropping a stone down a deep well. I pulled, and the bell answered, and the door was opened by a man. For the instant it seemed to me that I must have got to the wrong house. I had never seen Peter, and Rosie, taking it for granted that I had, never mentioned his appearance. But from the way we spoke of him I pictured him as a puffing corpulent little man. The Peter who opened the door was tall and spare, with a mad, melancholy face. He looked rather like Don Quixote. Before I had spoken he had shown me into a sitting-room—the one with the bow-window and the venetian blinds. It was dirty, cold, comfortless, and fusty, and seemed somehow random and disjected, as though at some time all the furniture had been violently disarranged and no one had troubled to put it straight again.

No one spoke. Peter stood behind me, and at the farther end of the room the two old women sat pressed together on a sofa. They sat embraced, each clasping the other's hand, as two children might have sat to be photographed sixty years ago, trembling with obedient stillness and staring at the black velvet cloth which hid the photographer. Mrs. Lecheminant had a purple bruise on the side of her face where I had hit her with the half-brick, and she nestled her head against her sister's bosom. Miss Perdew was tall, like Peter, and gaunt with ill usage and underfeeding.

I asked if Mrs. Flounders was at home. The answer, retarded like the answer of the door-bell, came from Miss Perdew.

"She's in her room. She has been there quite a long time. I think perhaps she is a little ill."

I said I would like to go to her. Neither sister spoke or moved.

Peter, behind me, plucked at my sleeve and whispered: "I'll show you. I'll show you. I know the way."

From the doorway I looked back at the old woman. I thought they had settled even more deeply into their abject embrace. Outside was Peter, grown animated. He capered up the stairs before me and along a passage where horns and antlers and crucifixes were fastened to the walls and up a second flight of stairs, and tapped on a door and without pausing opened it.

I saw a massive double-bed, set sideways against the wall. It had been slept in, but it was empty. I waited for some minutes, keeping Peter away. Then it occurred to me to touch the bed. It was cold.

"Warm, very warm," said Peter. "Shall we play Hunt the Thimble?"

There was a strip of carpet beside the bed and it was rumpled and lay askew. I stooped down and lifted the valance and looked. There was very little room between the base of the mattress and the floor but Rosie had contrived to squeeze in and roll herself against the wall. There was a lot of dust under the bed, her body had swept a track, she was covered with flue and cobwebs.

She had got there to be out of Peter's reach, and Peter's reach was considerably longer than mine. I turned on him and said: "I'll tell your father."

He shrank out of the room. Rosie's comparison with the soufflé was exactly true, and I wondered why she had not been able to quell him herself in the same way. Perhaps she had tried it too often. Perhaps she felt too ill. When I crawled in and touched her she was cold and stiff. So I crawled out again and sat down on the bed and wished with all my heart for Wangles.

After a while I pulled myself together again and went away, past Peter, who was standing in the antlered passage looking out of a window, past the door that had the two old women behind it, and reported what I had found. To spare Roderic's feelings and the good name of two highly respected local families, the inquest was limited to medical evidence, and Mrs. Rose Flounders, daughter of the late Henry Peverel Esq. and Mrs. Peverel, was found to have died of a cardiac condition, accelerated, the Coroner suggested, by her devoted work in the national effort, involving overstrain and exposure to climatic inclemencies. This may be partially true. Rosie was certainly drinking too much; if she had stayed at home moderately bitching instead of going on the road and keeping the weather out, I suppose she might still be alive, and Peter Perdew still at large (he is in an asylum now where his annuity pays for him; the two old women are in some sort of charitable hostel; the house is a nursing-home). But the real truth is that Rosie died through ambition—by which sin fell the angels.